RUNNING FROM LOVE

Paris Tyler

Love Swan
Books

Post Office Box 401170
San Francisco, CA 94140

Paris Tyler/Love Swan Books
PO Box 401170
San Francisco, CA 94140
www.loveswanbooks.com

Publisher's Note: This is a work of fiction. Names, characters, places, and incidents are a product of the author's imagination. Locales and public names are sometimes used for atmospheric purposes. Any resemblance to actual people, living or dead, or to businesses, companies, events, institutions, or locales is completely coincidental.

Cover Artwork by Sam Mayle © 2016
Book Layout © 2016 BookDesignTemplates.com

Running From Love/ Paris Tyler. -- 1st ed.
ISBN 978-0-9637683-0-8

My heartfelt thanks and gratitude to all that helped make this book a published work; too many to name here. And a special thank you to BJ who inspires me in more ways than he knows.

CHAPTER ONE

"You really shouldn't do it that way."

Lauren Evans felt irritation flare inside her at the interruption. As she looked up from the stretching she did every morning before she began her five mile run, her gaze strolled the length of well-toned, tanned legs. She mentally noted the strong, muscular chest and shoulders of the man in front of her before she connected with the deep midnight blue eyes of the tall stranger who had broken her concentration.

Lauren gasped. The man in front of her was gorgeous.

"Put your weight on this foot…" the stranger leaned down and grasped Lauren's ankle in his strong hand. Lauren was surprised at the electric response she felt at his touch. "Lean forward and support your weight here," the man continued as he indicated to Lauren the proper placement of her leg.

Lauren felt his warm, velvety voice wrap around her and she forced herself to concentrate on what the man was saying. She felt irritated that this stranger had interrupted the one time of the day she reserved for herself. She felt further irritation as she noticed that his alteration to her stretch did feel better and worked more effectively at lengthening her muscle.

"The strain on your muscle is lessened and you still get the same result." Lauren glared at the man in front of her, angry with him for interrupting her and angry with him for being right.

"Have a nice run." The tall, dark stranger stood up and sprinted away leaving Lauren feeling flustered. The skin on her leg that had been touched by his hand felt cold now that he was gone and Lauren tried to convince herself it was because it was a cool morning.

Lauren lived in Santa Barbara, a beautiful city with a Spanish motif nestled between the ocean and mountains along the coast of California. She had originally come out to Santa Barbara from the Midwest to attend the university and she had fallen in love with the city. After she graduated she had decided to stay. It was mornings like this one that made her feel like she lived in paradise. Mornings like this one minus the arrogant, know-it-all intruder.

She normally stretched by the harbor and ran the length of the beach to the bird sanctuary on the other side. This morning she only had time to run to the volleyball courts at East Beach and back. As she continued to stretch her tall, slender frame she saw other morning runners familiar to her daily routine.

She started to run. She took deep breaths of the early morning air to clear the last remains of sleep from her body. This was her peaceful time alone before she began her rigorous work as a paralegal at a local law firm. She glanced out at the water and could see the offshore oil rigs. With any luck, her firm would be able to deter future offshore drilling. Her office handled several cases to protect the environment. Lauren felt very strongly about preserving the Earth's resources and wildlife. The oil deposits in the sand along her path were only one sign of the havoc the drilling wreaked on the land. But still, it was a beautiful morning and even the drills could not distract Lauren from her feeling of contentment. The rhythm to her stride made her feel good.

The volleyball courts were coming up on the right. Almost time to turn back. Lauren looked at her watch and felt a twinge of regret that she would not be able to make it all the way to the bird sanctuary. She enjoyed looking at the wide variety of wildlife as she ran around the perimeter of the sanctuary before she started the run back to her home.

As Lauren neared the volleyball courts and turned to make her return, she saw the stranger again. Something about the way he ran made her catch her breath. She already knew he was very attractive, well-built and tall and that he was dressed in shorts and a t-shirt which exposed his tan, toned body. But nothing had prepared her for the wind that pressed his shirt against his stomach as he ran, accenting the washboard ripple of muscle underneath or the fluid grace of his stride.

He had dark, almost black hair and those deep blue eyes of his seemed to swallow her as she approached him. She could not help but notice his full, appreciative observation of her as she neared. She could feel her cheeks warm and felt a ripple of excitement pass through her body as he got closer.

"Hello, again," he said as he passed her. His voice sounded rich and deep.

"Hel...lo," Lauren faltered as her voice stuck in her throat. She must be more winded than she thought. Normally she never noticed men. Her focus was on her work and attending law school the following September.

Lauren had been dating Jim Adamson for several months and they had settled into a comfortable dating relationship. She wasn't interested in anything more than a friendly dating arrangement and he wasn't pressuring her.

It surprised Lauren that she reacted so strongly to this stranger. She was already dating someone, and even though she was free to date other people, Lauren felt it was more important to focus on her career.

Lauren returned to the harbor and slowed to a walking pace to cool down from her run. As she started the short walk back to her apartment she tried to put the mysterious runner out of her mind and focus instead on her upcoming work day.

This was the day a new attorney was coming to their office to assist with the Consumer Energy trial to deter future offshore oil drilling. Marcus Harland was considered an expert in environmental law. Although they had never met, Lauren knew that he was powerful and impressive in the courtroom. She had seen a newspaper article which chronicled a few of his many career successes and she knew that he had already established a formidable reputation even though he was still in his early thirties. What little Lauren knew about Marcus Harland's career made her anxious to meet him and start working with him. She was looking forward to the experience. After all, it was not every day that a paralegal was able to assist an attorney with Marcus Harland's reputation.

Lauren lived in a small cottage-style apartment several blocks from the beach. As she retrieved her apartment keys from the planter box and opened her front door her cat, Buster, meowed his greeting.

"How is my purr-boy today?" Lauren reached down and scratched Buster behind the ears. He answered her with a deep rumbling purr and brushed up against her slender legs. Lauren had found Buster outside her door one morning and he had adopted her from the start. He was a large, black and white cat with four white paws. He had obviously tackled a few of the neighborhood cats and had a diagonal scar across his nose to prove it.

Lauren had noticed that Buster, although very loving and gentle towards her, could be very protective when other people were around. Only now, after several months, did Buster accept Jim and still only with an aura of tolerance, not affection.

Lauren stripped off the black running shorts and red sport top she had been wearing and quickly showered. She dressed in a crisp, dark navy suit and cream colored silk blouse, both with a professional cut. Lauren had tried very hard to conceal her feminine features in an effort to be taken seriously at the law firm. Although women had been practicing law for quite some time, it was still a male dominated environment. It still amazed her that there was still a large gap between the sexes in the corporate environment. She looked forward to a time when things truly had changed. Until then she would do everything she could to perform in a professional manner and work at changing perceptions.

Lauren picked up the law book she had been reading the night before and put it into her briefcase, grabbed her purse and headed for the door. As she let Buster out, she called to him, "Don't bully the other cats today." She knew he did not understand much of what she said, but Lauren enjoyed talking to her cat. "I'll see you tonight when I get back from work."

Even though Lauren knew that Buster viewed her apartment as his home, there were still times when he would disappear for a few days, usually to re-appear with scratches from a fight. It always made her feel a little uneasy when he did not return after a day or two.

Lauren's office was located on State Street, the main thoroughfare in Santa Barbara. She lived to the west, within walking distance from her office. Even though she owned a little compact car, she enjoyed walking whenever she could. She used her car primarily for shopping and visiting her friend, Mariana, in Los Angeles, located several hours away.

Lauren made her way towards a large, Spanish style building. Santa Barbara consisted of many low-rise buildings because of strict building regulations. The law office of Whitman, Hawkins & Smythe was located in one of the few tall buildings downtown. As she entered the tiled lobby of the building she walked past a beautiful fountain with water cascading down several tiers. The fountain was the home to several koi and she occasionally saw people throwing coins into the water, presumably for luck. She loved the fountain because the gurgling sounds of the water made her feel she was near a brook, sounding similar to the river that ran behind her parent's home in Michigan where she grew up. She always felt a little nostalgic as she passed.

She waited for the elevator to take her to the top floor of the building. As Lauren pushed open the large, dark wooden doors marked 'Whitman, Hawkins & Smythe' she set her mind to the work ahead.

"Hello, Julie," Lauren greeted the receptionist, a young blond woman who had been with the firm for several months.

"Hi Lauren, here are your messages," she replied. "And, by the way, Leo was looking for you. He should be in his office right now."

Leo Whitman, one of the founding partners of the firm, was a gentle, older man. His once-brown hair was almost completely grey. Lauren had always found him to be a wonderful, supportive colleague whom she respected as a lawyer and a friend. She trusted his judgement and admired him. She had worked with him on several cases and always viewed him with awe in the courtroom. She saw him as a warm and compassionate man removed from the courtroom and completely determined and effective when he was inside one. Leo was a man of integrity and he always fought, as he would say, "for the right side."

"Ah...there you are Lauren, I trust you had a pleasant weekend?"

"Yes, Leo. I had the opportunity to review the history on the Consumer Energy case. If you'd like, I can give you the notes on my research."

Leo shook his head. He looked at the tall, auburn haired woman in front of him. What a beautiful woman, and all she ever did was work. He had met her boyfriend, Jim, and could not understand the attraction. *Oh well,* he thought, *she was bright and excellent at her job. She would be a very good attorney after she gets her degree.*

"Good, good. I'd like to take a look at those notes later, but first, I wanted to let you know that I spoke to Marcus Harland. He got into town yesterday. He will be meeting with a realtor this morning and I expect him to be here before lunch."

"I'm looking forward to meeting him, Leo," Lauren replied.

"Good, good. I'm counting on you to make a good impression of the firm. He's only here temporarily to work on the Consumer Energy case and I want him to feel comfortable during his stay. I'm entrusting you to show him the courthouse and fill him in on office procedures. Do you feel up to it?" Leo inquired.

"Of course. I should be in the law library for the majority of the morning, just let me know when he gets here," Lauren answered.

As Lauren made her way to the law library, she tried to envision Marcus Harland. Even though she knew he was thirty-three, she had a difficult time imagining him as anything but a bookworm. *Too bad there wasn't a photo of him with the article I read,* she thought. *If there had been one it would be easier to prepare for their meeting.* As it was, she only had a vague impression to associate with what little she knew of him. Well, it really didn't matter. He could be short and bald for all she cared.

Lauren pushed open one of the heavy glass doors that led into the law library. The room had a contemporary flair that seemed to contradict the heavy, leather-bound volumes that surrounded her. Large, sun-filled windows spread warmth throughout the room. In addition, several upholstered chairs created a sitting area that made the work environment more comfortable. Many times, Lauren found herself engrossed for several hours without noticing the time.

One of Lauren's responsibilities was to research a variety of case histories that might reflect precedence on the case to which she was currently assigned. She found reading the variety of cases intriguing and complex. She knew that Marcus Harland was mentioned throughout many of the case files. Lauren had read several of the entries and they only proved to further her interest in Mr. Harland. She had formed an opinion of him as a bookworm-type and someone who would be a valuable teacher.

Lauren worked throughout the morning, reading case histories and making notes on her legal pad. When she began to feel stiff from sitting for several hours and after having finishing reading the last case study in the law journal, she decided to stretch. She had taken off her suit jacket earlier and had placed it on the back of one of the chairs. Without the jacket to restrict her movement, she was able to stretch and give some relief to her tired muscles.

During her reading, one of the volumes had referenced a case she was not familiar with and she decided she had time to scan the entry before taking a break for lunch. The shelves were stacked from floor to ceiling with a variety of text books. The book she was interested in was located on one of the upper shelves. Although Lauren was tall she decided it would be better to stand on a chair to reach the book. She kicked off her high-heeled pumps and stood on the seat of the chair and strained to reach the volume. As she extended her arm she could feel the skirt of her suit cling to the sides of her body. The lines of the suit were able to hide her feminine curves the majority of the time, but as she leaned over the chair the skirt only emphasized her feminine figure. The book was only several inches away and as she reached for the volume she could hear the heavy glass doors swish open as someone entered the law library.

"Ah...there you are, Lauren," Leo looked up as he entered the room. "I'd like to introduce you to Marcus Harland."

As she turned to answer, her green-gold eyes fell into a deep sea of midnight blue as her gaze locked with the most intense eyes she had ever seen. Lauren had seen eyes like them only once before.

It felt like an eternity before Lauren was able to break away from the gaze that returned her stare with equal intensity. She had to steady herself as she stepped down from the chair and she felt awkward and clumsy as she made her way over to the two men. She felt at a disadvantage without her shoes, which were still lying discarded by the chair.

She could feel her cheeks warm as she thought of how she'd been standing on the chair. She felt embarrassed being caught in such an unprofessional position.

"Well, we meet again," a cool and luxurious voice greeted her.

"Oh, I didn't realize you two had already met," interjected Leo.

"Well, not exactly. Our paths crossed this morning when I was running along the beach." Lauren turned to Marcus Harland and, as she spoke she was amazed to hear how calm and poised she sounded. "I'm Lauren Evans. It is very nice to meet you, Mr. Harland," she said as she extended her hand.

Before she could continue he interrupted her, "Please, call me Marc. We are going to be working together on the Consumer Energy case for several months. I'd say that calls for a more informal work environment."

Lauren was convinced she saw his eyes flicker towards the chair she had just abandoned as he reached out his hand. At least he wasn't holding her previous precarious position against her. Her initial fears that he would judge her behavior as unprofessional evaporated. She tried not to think about the incident by the beach.

As he took her hand, Lauren was amazed at how this powerful man who loomed above her could have a grasp that was both strong and gentle at the same time. She felt a twinge of current run through her arm. At his close proximity, she was able to take in more of his features than she had been able to earlier that morning on the beach.

Marc Harland could be described as a beautiful man with the exception of a rough edge about him that was very masculine. Lauren decided it was his determined jaw that hardened the beauty. He stood well over six feet tall and even with her generous height of 5'9", Lauren felt dwarfed. His hair was almost black and Lauren noticed a few grey hairs scattered throughout. His eyes were his most captivating feature, dark blue like the depths of the ocean. A dark, very expensive suit, white shirt and suspenders had replaced his running attire.

At the moment his eyes were viewing her with a mixture of humor and expectancy and Lauren realized that she had been staring again. What was it about this man? First along the beach and again now. If she only could have had the advantage of the several inches her shoes would have provided, then maybe she would feel more his equal.

Leo broke through her rapture. "Marc, I've asked Lauren to help you find your way around. She'll show you the courthouse and get you settled in."

Marc's eyes never broke contact with hers as he replied, "I look forward to it." Lauren felt another flush of color warm her cheeks.

"It's no trouble, really," Lauren replied hastily. "If you'd like, we can go to the courthouse later this afternoon."

"Well, Marc, you are in capable hands. I need to get to a meeting, but Lauren, why don't you take Marc to lunch and then go to the courthouse. That is, if you don't already have lunch plans?"

"Well...no." The last thing Lauren wanted was to be alone with this man who made her senses reel. She felt like a young schoolgirl and didn't like it. She was a professional woman and no man was going to make her feel inadequate. He was probably one of those men that thought women should be at home tending to housework. "Actually, I was just about to read a few more entries that were pertinent to the case."

"Good, good," Leo replied, "but surely that can wait until after lunch. Why don't you take Marc to that wonderful little cafe up the street? Show him a little of what our city has to offer." And with that, Leo left the two of them standing in the library.

"Well, let me take a minute to straighten up in here." Lauren immediately felt her clumsiness reappear as she tried to stack books and return them to their proper shelves. She could feel those deep blue eyes watching her and when he made no effort to respond she turned, "You don't mind, do you?"

"No, not at all. If you'll hand me a few of the volumes, I can help you re-shelve." There was that smooth, deep voice again. Lauren released a sigh as she handed over several of the volumes. It was the first time she felt he was not looking deep inside her as she watched him move around the library shelving books. He had strong, neat hands that gripped the books with ease and he moved with the grace of a lean and powerful man who was comfortable with himself. Within minutes they were able to return all the books to the proper shelf locations.

"Leo suggested the cafe up the street, which has great sandwiches and salads, or, if you'd prefer, we can get something else."

"No, sandwiches sound fine, Lauren. May I call you Lauren?" Marc asked casually. The way he said her name sounded musical.

"Yes, that's fine," Lauren replied as she clumsily tried to slip her feet back into her shoes. Marc picked up her discarded suit jacket and held it up for her to put on. His fingers brushed the thin silk blouse she wore as she slipped into the jacket and she felt his breath on the back of her neck. The action of helping her into her jacket had taken on an air of intimacy that left Lauren feeling flustered. She felt an urgent need to get away from this man, away from his deep blue eyes, away from his strong, lean hands.

As they walked towards the door of the library, Lauren noticed that he was still several inches taller than she was even with the added inches of height her shoes provided.

The cafe was charming and was beginning to fill with the usual downtown lunch crowd. The hostess led them to a patio table that provided a view of the street as well as the plant filled interior of the restaurant. As they reviewed their menus, Lauren was aware of the silence that ensued. It was pleasant and not at all uncomfortable, but Lauren felt her nerves were being stretched by his close proximity. She shouldn't have stayed up so late reading the night before. She must be overtired.

"Tell me, how long have you been with the firm, Lauren?" Marc asked as he closed his menu and focused his attention on her.

"A little over three years. Leo hired me after I graduated from the university," Lauren replied. Inwardly she wanted to kick herself. She didn't want him to think she was inexperienced and young. She was aware that some of the attorneys at the firm viewed her as being "green" because she was only twenty-four. She worked hard at her job and she realized how important it was to her to have Marc Harland acknowledge her abilities. But he wasn't looking at her with any emotion other than interest. His eyes didn't reveal the patronizing look she had seen on other occasions. Her admission didn't even make him blink.

"What did you study at the university?"

"Political Science and no, before you ask, I have no political aspirations. I've always known I wanted to be an attorney."

Marc Harland leaned back in his chair and his eyes glinted good-naturedly. "So what's holding you back? Why are you working as a paralegal?"

Lauren could feel herself bristle. Her job was very important to her and she could feel the subtle reference to "only a paralegal." She had run into that attitude before. Looking at his dark, well-tailored suit she guessed he had never lacked for anything in his life. For her though, as the daughter of kind and wonderful parents who had been able to give her much love but not much financial support when it came to college, getting her law degree was not quite as easy. For the last three years she had been saving diligently for her additional schooling and her hard work was beginning to pay off. Leo Whitman had already approached her about working part-time to subsidize her education and had hinted at offering her an associate position upon passing the Bar. Lauren was a very proud woman and getting through law school without incurring much debt was very important to her.

"Actually," Lauren answered curtly, "I've applied and been accepted into two different law programs. One is here in Santa Barbara through the university and the other is at a university in Michigan near my parents' home in Ann Arbor. I will be starting this fall." Lauren didn't tell him that she'd been having trouble deciding which program to attend. She felt a strong desire to stay in Santa Barbara and accept Leo's offer of a part-time position at the firm while she was studying. She felt that staying would be her best career choice, but she also felt that she should be near her parents, as they were getting older. It was a dilemma she would have to resolve soon.

"Both programs sound very good. Congratulations." Lauren knew from the article that she'd read that Marc had received his law degree from a prestigious school in Boston.

When the waiter appeared, Marc said, "Have you decided what you'd like for lunch?"

As Lauren ordered a Cobb salad and an iced tea, she tried to get her emotions in check. This morning she'd thought he was arrogant. During lunch she had become defensive when Marc started questioning her, but his reactions to her answers reflected sincere interest. Part of her found him maddening and, although she did not want to admit it to herself, another part of her was attracted to him.

"I'll have the steak sandwich," Marc said as he turned to the waiter. "And, an iced tea sounds refreshing."

Marcus Harland had been hired to work on the pre-trial preparations of the Consumer Energy case and represent the firm in court when the case went to trial in several weeks. Although the case had several complexities, it was expected that the time Marc Harland would be at Whitman, Hawkins & Smythe would be around three months, enough time to complete his obligations.

Lauren knew that Marc had been approached by many firms offering him a position, but as she found out over lunch, he felt he had a better opportunity to develop his expertise if he focused entirely on environmental law. Settling down with one law firm would require him to work on a variety of cases.

"Where were you before you came to our firm?" Lauren asked as she munched on her salad.

"I was working up in San Francisco, specifically on a case protecting the wildlife of the bay. A lot of the animals that have their homes in or around the bay have been forced North or South due to increased manufacturing. Several species have even been endangered. We were working on creating habitats that protect them within their natural surroundings."

"How did you become interested in environmental law?" Lauren asked as she reached for her iced tea. Inside, her emotions were churning and she hoped she would be able to keep the conversation at an impersonal level.

"Actually, when I graduated from law school my intention was to become a corporate attorney and pursue the almighty dollar."

That fits, Lauren thought to herself as she looked at the powerful man in front of her, dressed in an expensive suit.

"I actually landed a job with a large oil corporation in Texas. There was a lot of corporate work and I was convinced I had found my dream job." Lauren felt Marc's voice wrap around her as he spoke.

"To make a long story short, one of the programs started by the corporation was established to protect the wildlife around the oil drilling sites. That's how I got involved in environmental law." It surprised Lauren that

Marc could have been a corporate attorney and been motivated to change the environmental world.

"I ended up leaving the company so that I could focus entirely on environmental issues," Marc concluded. His career path conveyed a sensitivity that Lauren was not ready to acknowledge or accept.

As they continued their discussion Lauren noticed that Marc spoke with a casualness that contradicted his powerful image. But Lauren saw a steely determination that was always present when Marc spoke about his work. He was a man who knew exactly what he wanted and did everything to get it, Lauren concluded.

"What about you, Lauren. What prompted you to get involved with environmental issues?"

"Birds."

"Birds?"

Lauren felt a wave of shyness wash over her with the intensity of Marc's blue gaze. "I'm sure you've seen birds that have been covered in crude oil. They can't fly and their lives are cut short. That was the first time I realized that we live in an intertwined world. Our actions really affect everything around us."

Lauren could tell by their luncheon conversation that Marc would not be staying with the firm after the case was completed, even though she knew Leo had offered Marc the opportunity to take the Consumer Energy case to court in an effort to lure him to stay with the firm once it was completed.

Lauren convinced herself that the friendly, approachable man in front of her could not be for real. Marcus Harland had to be used to getting everything he wanted and Lauren decided that acting was just part of the job. She did not want to admit it, but she saw a part of herself in the man in front of her; the part that was passionate about an issue. Instead she tried to coerce herself into thinking that he had to have selfish motivations.

Throughout their lunch, by concentrating on their conversation and not on Marc physically, Lauren was able to keep her emotions in check. As they stood up to leave the cafe, Marc placed his hand on her elbow to help guide her between the tables and Lauren felt like her feet developed a mind of their own. Her unsteady balance only made Marc strengthen his hold on her arm, which only compounded the problem. If she could only get away from this man, away from his sexy charm and away from the look of steely determination that glinted in his dark blue eyes. Suddenly three months seemed like a very long time.

Luckily they were soon outside of the restaurant and Marc let his hand fall. "Which way to the courthouse?" he asked and Lauren led the way.

CHAPTER TWO

Lauren and Marc walked the few blocks to the Santa Barbara courthouse, a beautiful Spanish style building constructed on a complete city block during the late nineteen-twenties. The building was impressive with a fountain in front and an archway that led to large sunken gardens in the back. Many residents came to have picnics in the gardens and it was not uncommon to see people getting married outside.

Lauren led Marc towards the south entrance and they wound their way up a spiral, tiled staircase to the upper level. At the top of the stairs was the County Recorder's office where all pre-trial documents were filed. There was also a reference section with listings of small business names and pending cases.

Lauren introduced Marc to the three different clerks at the Recorder's office. She could not help but notice the suggestive glances that Sarah, one of the clerks, gave him. Lauren doubted that Marc lacked female attention. That fact alone made her want to have nothing to do with this man. She had no interest in being another notch on a bedpost somewhere.

Lauren mentally shook herself. She could almost feel the imprint of Marc's hand where he had touched her earlier that day. Lauren scolded herself. He had touched her casually showing her the proper stretch. His touch had not been intimate.

What was she thinking? Marc hadn't suggested any type of interlude with her. He'd treated her in nothing but a professional, cordial manner since they'd met at the firm. As Lauren watched him with Sarah, she felt a twinge of regret that it wasn't her that was getting his attention. *This is silly*, she thought. *I don't even know the man and I'm not interested even if I did.* Lauren tried to remember how irritated she'd felt at the beach. She tried to tell herself that this man was arrogant and had interrupted her private time.

They continued their tour and Lauren noticed that the majority of women responded favorably to Marc. From the young clerks to the more matronly judicial secretaries, Marc handled each one with grace and charm. Lauren could hardly believe it. Did they not see that he was just smooth, a man whose job required him to be manipulative and convincing? He wasn't going to be in Santa Barbara long, certainly not long enough to establish any relationships. He was probably used to getting everything he wanted, even jobs at firms he had no intention of joining.

Lauren kept reminding herself that he would only be here for three months. Only three months of having her life and job turned upside down.

Lauren opened the door to her apartment and dropped her keys onto the entry table next to a centerpiece of flowers that had been fresher a few days earlier. It was almost six-thirty and she only had thirty minutes to unwind and get ready for her dinner date with Jim.

It had seemed like the afternoon would never end. After the courthouse tour, Lauren and Marc had returned to the office and had spent the remainder of the day reviewing the Consumer Energy case files.

Lauren realized she was still standing at the entry to her apartment and she vowed to put Marcus Harland out of her mind. She kicked off her pumps and leaned down to pick them up as she made her way to her bedroom to change.

She selected a floral, sleeveless sundress that was form fitting to her waist and flared at her hips down to the lower part of her calves. She slipped into a pair of flat sandals and slung a turquoise colored sweater over her shoulders for later when the Santa Barbara air would become cooler.

After Lauren finished dressing she went to the back door of her apartment and looked for Buster. He was sitting on the back step and greeted her by brushing against her leg when she opened the door to let him in. She mixed wet and dry cat food on a plate and put it down on the floor for him to enjoy.

Several minutes after seven o'clock the doorbell rang and Lauren walked to the front door. Jim Adamson was an average looking blond man with nondescript features. He stood about an inch taller than Lauren and, although he had never said anything, she always tried to wear flat shoes when they were together.

"Ready?" Jim asked, as he absentmindedly brushed her cheek with his lips. "I've had a long day and all I want to do is get a drink. How 'bout going to the Fish Shack down by the wharf?"

"Sure, that sounds fine." Lauren picked up her purse as Jim impatiently shifted his weight from one foot to the other. Lauren thought he looked uncomfortable as he stood before her.

Jim ordered a scotch as soon as they were seated at their small table with an ocean view. Lauren usually enjoyed coming to the Fish Shack. The food was good and she liked to watch the sailboats returning to the harbor as the sun was setting. But tonight Jim complained about his day and about the service and he had ordered several additional drinks before the evening ended.

When the meal was finally over, they walked back to her apartment. Jim leaned over and gave her a prosaic kiss on the mouth. Lauren could taste the scotch on his breath.

"Do you want to come in for coffee?" Lauren asked. Jim was too intoxicated to drive home and Lauren hoped the coffee would help sober him.

As soon as they entered her apartment, Lauren headed to the kitchen and started brewing a strong Colombian coffee. Jim settled down onto the couch in the living room and started flipping through one of the magazines on the coffee table.

"The attorney I told you about who is taking the Consumer Energy case to trial came to the office today," Lauren started. It was the first time all evening that she was able to relay any information about her day. "His name is Marc Harland. I think he'll do a great job on the trial, but he seems a little, I don't know... arrogant might be the word I'm looking for."

"Sounds like a typical attorney to me," Jim replied. His response made Lauren cringe. Sometimes she wondered if Jim realized she was on her way to becoming an attorney. It made her wonder how Jim viewed her and her career choice. She didn't agree with him that arrogance was a classic characteristic of lawyers. Leo was a perfect example. Leo could hardly be termed as arrogant.

Lauren carried in a tray with a full coffee pot, two mugs and a plate of Italian dipping cookies into the living room. "Arrogant may not be the right word, Jim, it's just that Marc Harland made me feel uncomfortable. I'm not sure how I feel about him." As Lauren poured the coffee, she wished that Jim was a little more understanding about her career. All evening he'd been self-absorbed with his own work day, never thinking to inquire about hers.

Jim tossed the magazine back onto the table. "Look Lauren, I'm sure this guy is going to be alright. You're just being too sensitive. Anyway, I want to talk to you about something more important." As he was speaking, Jim moved closer to Lauren and put his arm around her shoulders.

Lauren cringed again. Why did he always dismiss her feelings? He never paid attention to how she felt. She had wanted to discuss her day at the office and the uneasiness she felt about Marc Harland. Lauren sighed. Apparently Jim wasn't able to understand.

"Look, honey, we have been dating awhile now and I think it's time that we considered where we want to go with this relationship. I haven't pressured you because I thought you needed time, but I want you to know I want more... that I need more...than a kiss at the door," Jim said.

Lauren sat completely still. *How romantic*, she thought sarcastically. She was a practical person and so was Jim. Maybe it made sense that any physical proposal would be made in a practical manner, from one practical person to another.

Jim took her silence as a sign of acceptance and leaned over to kiss her. He kissed her and started to push her down on the couch. Lauren felt suffocated and confused as she reached up to push Jim away.

"I need a little more time." The smell of alcohol was strong between them.

"How much more time do you need? I've already waited a long time," Jim interrupted, angrily. He tried to kiss her again, his hands digging into her shoulders.

"Jim, you've been drinking," Lauren retorted, her own anger flaring. "I'm not ready for this. I need time to think about it and if that's not good enough, get out!" Lauren struggled free and walked to the door, yanking it open. She stood there defiantly, gripping the doorknob so hard she started to lose the feeling in her hand.

"Awe, come on honey..." Jim said as he sauntered over to her, ignoring all the signals her body was projecting. "I'm only human...come on." He drunkenly swooped to her neck and kissed her at the base of her throat. Lauren felt a rise of panic as she pushed him away. This was not the Jim she knew, this was a drunken Jim and she wanted no part of him. Her concern for him driving was intensified. It was obvious he shouldn't be driving and she hesitated before she let go of the doorknob, torn between her urge to throw him out and concern for his safety.

"Stay there," she ordered him as she picked up the phone and called a cab. It seemed like an eternity before the cab arrived and she was able to tuck Jim into the back seat and give the driver the address to Jim's apartment. It had registered with Jim, somewhat belatedly, that Lauren still needed time. Before the cab pulled away, he asked, "Just think about it, alright?"

Lauren closed and locked the door behind her as she re-entered her apartment. It had been a long day, and it took all of her remaining energy to get ready for bed. She fell asleep almost as soon as her head hit the pillow. She was able to sleep the majority of the night through, but she dreamt images of Marc Harland and Jim Adamson. Both men represented turmoil and conflict in her life and she woke early in the morning to a feeling of apprehension. Apparently she wasn't going to get any more sleep, and Lauren decided to get up and prepare for her day.

Lauren completed her run quickly, hardly taking the time to notice other runners and scenery around her. When she returned to her apartment she showered and changed into her work clothes and was able to make it into the office before seven a.m. She headed to her office and put her purse in the lower drawer of her desk and made her way to the law library. It was early enough that she had the office all to herself.

The books provided comfort and reading soothed her rattled nerves. Around ten o'clock she decided to take a break and ran into Julie in the hallway. Julie greeted her with her messages and a giggling grin.

"What is it? What's so funny?" Lauren asked as she flipped through her messages.

"Oh...nothing, really. Just look in your office, you just got a delivery." Julie replied.

Lauren made her way down the hall to her office wondering what delivery had arrived. Twelve beautiful, red roses were in a vase on top of her desk. Lauren smelled them as she reached for the card.

The note was short; "Promise me you'll think about my proposal, Jim."

Well the flowers make him a little more romantic, Lauren thought as she read the card. *But I would hardly call an offer to share a bed a 'proposal'.* She tossed the card onto her desk and headed for the office kitchenette to get some hot tea before she went back to the law library.

Marc Harland was sitting at the table when she returned with her tea and she pulled up a chair to join him.

"Good morning, Lauren. You started early this morning from the look of these books," Marc greeted her.

"I thought I would read a few more case histories this morning. If you'd like, we can go over my findings this afternoon," Lauren explained after she wished him a good morning.

Marc Harland leaned back in his chair. His eyes registered the professional cut of her suit and silk blouse before he raised them to meet her gaze. He remembered the way she looked when he had walked into the law library the day before.

He'd seen a beautiful woman precariously balanced on a chair. She'd had a unique quality about her, but she had also seemed familiar to him. Only when she'd turned to face him had Marc realized that she was the same woman from the beach. Her delicate ankle had left a searing sensation on his hand when he'd touched her and he could almost feel the sensation return as he'd looked at her.

Marc noticed she looked tired today. Her face was drawn and pale. "I'd like to look over your report. I've been reading the case files and they are very interesting. I think we have several different angles to pursue. Have a seat, I'll fill you in."

Marc and Lauren sat together for the majority of the morning working over the case files. Marc had incredible energy and when Lauren finally got up to get herself some more tea she felt a sense of accomplishment at the work they'd completed together. She had begun to develop a sense of admiration for Marcus Harland, the attorney. She realized his reputation was well deserved and yet she still had reservations about Marcus Harland, the man.

"You've got a great eye for detail. I think we're going to be a good pair," Marc interrupted her thoughts. Lauren could feel herself blush under his scrutiny, his eyes locking with hers as she tried to ignore the innuendo in his voice as he stood close to her.

"Come on, I'll buy you lunch. You certainly deserve it after this morning," Marc continued, his voice breaking the sexual tension that had developed between them.

Lauren turned her head to one side as she looked at the man in front of her. It looked like Marc had complete control over his emotions, unlike Lauren. She watched him move away as he started re-shelving books. She was still struggling to suppress the excitement that had flared up inside her in response to his silky voice. He had been standing close enough to her to give the illusion that he had touched her with more than his voice.

The excitement Lauren felt was unlike anything she had experienced before. No wonder she felt a sense of apprehension where Marc Harland was concerned. It wasn't so much whether or not she could trust him but whether or not she could trust herself.

"I have to get my purse from my office," Lauren said. "I'll meet you by the elevator."

"I'm ready to go now, why don't I tag along to your office with you and we'll go together," Marc answered.

"Because I want a minute to get my wits about me," Lauren thought warily. But without making a big issue, she realized she would have to accept his company.

The phone was ringing as she entered her office, and she answered it as she opened the bottom drawer of her desk and extracted her purse. "Lauren Evans."

"Hi Lauren, it's Jim."

The flowers! She hadn't called Jim to thank him for the flowers, but Lauren had been feeling uncomfortable about the previous evening. It was obvious from Jim's card that he hadn't felt that there was a reason to apologize for his behavior the night before. He was also pushing her towards something she wasn't ready for. Their relationship had been pleasant and comfortable until now. Why did he feel the sudden urge to change everything? She thought she'd been very clear about her involvement and expectations.

"Jim, thank you, the flowers are beautiful. Unfortunately though, I can't talk right now. Marc Harland and I are about to get something for lunch and I don't want to keep him waiting." Lauren glanced at Marc as she was talking into the phone. He was eyeing the flowers and his gaze fell upon the card on her desk.

"Well, alright Lauren. I guess it's fine to keep me waiting, but I certainly wouldn't want you to keep Marcus Harland waiting," Jim said sarcastically. "Call me later if you have some time. I want to talk to you about last night."

Lauren said goodbye and hung up the phone. She wondered if his behavior the night before was a result of a difficult day at the office and several drinks at dinner. Jim normally didn't drink more than an occasional beer or glass of wine and his behavior the previous evening hadn't been consistent with the Jim she knew. She hoped that everything would work out. She valued their relationship and didn't want to be forced into a corner that would inevitably cause problems between them.

Lauren was glad it appeared that Marc hadn't been very interested in the flowers or her conversation with Jim. She would have been embarrassed at displaying her personal life any more than she already had in front of a man she hardly knew.

Marc, however, had noticed the flowers and the card. He was surprised at the sudden feelings of jealousy that had flared inside him. He hardly knew Lauren and although he found her to be a beautiful and intriguing woman, it was obvious she was already involved in a relationship. How could he be feeling jealous when he hardly knew her? He couldn't help but notice, though, that the card and call both reflected unwillingness on Lauren's part to make a final commitment. Obviously she hadn't accepted Jim's proposal and the other man had sent flowers and called in an effort to persuade her. Somehow this knowledge gave Marc a sense of hope. *This is crazy,* Marc thought. *I'm only here for several months and then I'm gone. I don't want a relationship and this woman hardly seems like the type for a brief affair.*

Lauren and Marc left the office and waited for the elevator to arrive.

"There's a fun little bistro down the street. Do you like French food?" Lauren asked as the elevator bell rang.

"I love French food. That and Italian are my favorites," Marc responded.

Lauren laughed. "Mine, too! We'll have to try Italian next time." Lauren had overcome the initial feelings of apprehension concerning Marc Harland as a colleague. While working with him she'd realized that he was very capable. Her initial fears that he would view her as a woman who should be working as a legal secretary, or better yet, outside of the legal profession altogether, were gone. It was obvious that he viewed her as an equal co-worker. He'd been very complimentary after reviewing her research on the Consumer Energy case.

The elevator doors opened and the car was full of people presumably on their way to lunch as well. Several people shifted to allow Marc and Lauren to enter the elevator. In the tight quarters, Lauren was forced to stand very close to Marc and she could feel the heat of his body and smell the faint spicy scent of his aftershave.

Marc looked down at her and caught her gaze. Lauren felt unable to break the connection between them and wished she could lean closer. She wanted to inhale deeply and savor the scent of him. Luckily, the elevator reached the lobby and the push of people behind them broke their gazes and pushed them apart.

Lauren and Marc had an enjoyable lunch at the bistro around the corner. The food was wonderful and Lauren ended her meal with crème caramel, one of her personal favorites.

"You really should come here one evening for dinner. And make sure you order the chocolate soufflé," Lauren told Marc as she scooped up her dessert. "The soufflé is my favorite, but you need to call ahead to get it."

Marc enjoyed watching Lauren eat her food. She truly looked like she savored every mouthful. "Most women I know only shift food around on their plates and call it a meal," Marc commented.

"Well, I run every day, and that helps me have a healthy appetite," Lauren answered as she scraped the last remains of her dessert out of the fluted dish.

"Do you always run along the beach?"

"Pretty much. I like all the activity. Even running the same path every day is different when I run down by the water. There's always someone around doing something."

"Do you mind if I join you tomorrow?"

Lauren hesitated. She viewed her running time as the one portion of her day that was entirely for herself. "Do you think you can keep pace? I usually run about five miles."

"Well, I'm up for the challenge," replied Marc, his eyes sparkling.

"Alright, but I warn you, it's not a picnic. I am serious about my running. If you can't keep up I won't wait," Lauren warned.

"Fair enough," laughed Marc.

Lauren and Marc made their way back to the office and worked in the firm's library until late afternoon. Marc stood up and closed the case file he had been reading. "Well, I have to go. I've found an apartment and I'm moving my things out of the hotel."

"Where shall we meet tomorrow for the run?" Lauren made arrangements to meet Marc by the harbor and went to her office.

Lauren sat at her desk, viewing the flowers with a scowl on her face. She had to call Jim and talk to him about the night before. And he still needed to come by her apartment to get his car. She didn't know what to tell Jim and she hesitated to pick up the phone and initiate the call.

Lauren's parents had married shortly after they had met and Lauren had always felt her mother had compromised her life to accommodate her father's needs. Lauren believed her mother had never pursued her dreams and aspirations and, although she knew her mother was happy and content with the life she had chosen, Lauren knew that she herself needed more.

Lauren didn't want to get physically involved with Jim and risk a compromise between her career and relationship. Jim had not hidden the fact that he wanted a wife that would stay home with his children. Also, Lauren felt that any physical involvement should have emotional involvement as well, and even though she liked Jim and cared for him, she knew she wasn't in love with him.

Lauren picked up the phone and dialed Jim's number. He answered after a few rings and Lauren quickly arranged to pick him up at his office and take him to his car at her apartment. She hung up after promising to discuss the previous evening when she met with him. After retrieving her purse and keys, she headed to catch the elevator.

CHAPTER THREE

It took Lauren longer than she had anticipated to leave the office and walk the few blocks to her apartment to get her car. Jim was waiting at the corner, pacing impatiently as he watched Lauren drive up. He opened the car door when she pulled up to the curb and got into the passenger seat next to her. They drove along in silence for the first few blocks after exchanging normal, somewhat stilted pleasantries.

"I've been thinking about last night, what I can remember of it at least, and I, er, I just wanted to say I didn't handle the situation very well," started Jim.

Lauren didn't know how to respond. She was glad to hear that he recognized he had behaved badly; however, she felt that by accepting his apology she was not holding him accountable for his actions. "Just make sure something like that never happens again," Lauren started. "I mean... Jim, I care about you and I want you to be happy, but I refuse to be rushed into making a decision I'm not ready to make."

"All I'm asking, Lauren, is that you think about it. I'm not made of stone, you know," Jim answered.

"Alright, Jim," Lauren replied. She was thinking to herself that maybe she would be able to love Jim one day. People didn't fall in love at first sight like they did in the movies. Caring for and loving a person had to take time, Lauren rationalized.

With a common understanding of the events of the night before and the expectations each of them had, Lauren and Jim decided to go out to dinner. They chose a fun but trendy restaurant on the main strip of downtown.

Lauren and Jim were seated at a front table near the hostess podium and front entrance. The restaurant was beginning to fill with groups of people and as Lauren looked over her menu the noise level in the restaurant began to rise. Plates were clattering, people were talking and the hostess was successfully juggling a ringing telephone while people arrived to be seated for dinner.

Lauren and Jim had just finished ordering when Lauren noticed the door to the restaurant open and two people walk in and approach the hostess. The woman was a beautiful blond, probably in her late twenties. She was dressed in a pale colored linen suit and cream colored shoes. Lauren envied the woman's polished appearance. After a long day at the office Lauren was feeling a little disheveled.

It took Lauren by surprise to notice that the blonde's companion was Marc Harland. They were busy checking with the hostess for a table. Apparently they were being told it was going to be a few minutes because Marc turned with his companion to find seating in the lobby area. The restaurant was open and airy and Lauren had a clear view of Marc. As he turned, he saw Lauren and waved. She waved back and Marc headed over towards their table with his hand at the small of the blonde's back, guiding her towards them as well.

"That's Marc Harland, the new attorney at the office," Lauren said to Jim as the two approached.

"Hi, Lauren..." Marc said. "How was your dinner?"

"Actually we just ordered," Lauren replied. "Marc, I'd like you to meet Jim Adamson," Lauren continued.

"Very nice to meet you, Jim. This is Sylvia Lewis... Sylvia, this is Lauren Evans and Jim Adamson. Lauren and I work together," Marc said graciously.

The hostess made her way over to the table. "Mr. Harland, there's a table ready for you, or would you like to join your friends this evening?" The hostess had mistaken their exchange. Before Marc had a chance to reply, Jim was gesturing to the two additional chairs at their table.

"Please, consider joining us. We've just ordered. I'm sure our waitress can add your order to ours." Lauren was surprised by Jim's gesture.

Sylvia and Marc exchanged looks and Marc pulled out a chair, "We'd enjoy that very much."

They had a pleasant meal together. Lauren found out that Sylvia was the real estate agent who had found Marc's apartment for him. "This is our dinner to celebrate our success," Sylvia said, as she patted Marc's hand from across the table. It was obvious to Lauren that Sylvia hoped to find more than an apartment with Marc. It appeared that Marc hadn't wasted any time finding female companionship.

After dinner the waitress brought the bill to the table and Marc reached for it immediately. Jim made a slight attempt to help out with the bill, but Marc insisted on picking up the entire check. After the receipt had been brought back to the table and a tip left, the four of them stood up to leave.

"Thank you for a wonderful evening, Marc," Lauren said. "I had a very nice time. It was nice meeting you, Sylvia," Lauren continued as she turned toward the other woman. "I'll see you tomorrow morning, Marc."

"Bright and early," Marc responded and he and Sylvia turned to leave. Lauren and Jim left the restaurant after the other two and headed for her car.

"I don't like that man," said Jim. "Did you see how he picked up the tab for the entire table?"

Lauren felt herself get defensive. Why did she feel the sudden need to defend Marc Harland? "I thought it was a very kind gesture," replied Lauren. "I think he is a generous man." Lauren was surprised to realize that within a very short time her opinion of Marc Harland had changed. First she had begun to develop respect for his work and now, after sharing several meals with him, she realized she was beginning to develop respect for the man himself.

"Well, I think you were right yesterday. I think arrogant is the right word for him," Jim answered. "Picking up the tab for the entire meal was expensive. I don't know who he is trying to impress. I think he's just show off his success," Jim growled.

Lauren decided to remain quiet. It was obvious that Jim wasn't interested in hearing any opinion other than his own. She was beginning to realize just how often that was true.

Lauren drove Jim to his car and let him out just before she got to her driveway. He turned to her briefly and gave her a light kiss on the mouth before he got out of the car. "I'll talk to you soon, Lauren," he said before he shut the door of her car.

Lauren felt tired as she pulled her car into the carport behind her apartment. As she went in through the back door, she realized that Buster wasn't around. *Maybe he'll be back in the morning,* she thought. Regardless, Lauren left a dish of food and water on the back step in case he returned during the night.

She had had an enjoyable evening, but it was still early in the week and she had a lot to do at work before the weekend arrived. She began to undress as she made her way into her bedroom. Her pine, four-poster bed, covered in crisp white cotton sheets with eyelet embroidery and large, plush pillows, looked inviting. After undressing and taking a quick bath, Lauren curled up in bed. She was asleep almost immediately.

Lauren woke to her alarm clock humming incessantly next to her. She looked at the time and realized she'd slept through the alarm for several minutes. She was feeling very relaxed and realized that it had been several nights since she'd been able to sleep the entire night through.

Remembering that she had to meet Marc in a few minutes, Lauren bolted out of bed. She dressed quickly in black shorts and covered them with a short white running top. She pulled on heavy white socks and her running shoes and headed for the door. She pulled her hair back with an elastic tie and then locked her front door, placing the keys in the flower box as she did every morning.

Lauren made her way to the harbor and looked around for Marc. She didn't see him anywhere and she started to stretch, preparing for her run. Bending over to stretch out her calf muscles, she grasped her ankles and counted out the stretch. Then she bent one leg and extended her other leg behind her and counted out the stretch and repeated the same movement stretching her other leg.

Lauren was in the process of doing side stretches when she saw Marc approach. He was wearing a simple white t-shirt that clung to his muscular frame and athletic shorts with a university logo. His legs were long and muscular, lightly covered with dark hair. "Is running the only exercise that you do?" Lauren blurted out, realizing after she spoke that she could not imagine that anyone could be in such excellent physical shape by only running.

"Good morning, Lauren," Marc said with a twinkle of humor in his voice and Lauren realized how crass she'd been. She could feel her cheeks warm as he continued. "Actually, I also do a little sailing. Maybe you would like to join me sometime."

"Maybe," Lauren answered as she concentrated on her stretching. She decided to get down to the business at hand. "I usually run along the length of the beach and back after circling around the bird sanctuary. It works out to be just over five miles. Is that too far for you?"

"I'll see how I do," Marc replied as he started to stretch. Lauren felt mesmerized as she watched him moving gracefully in front of her. She resumed her own stretching and tried not to look at the man in front of her.

When they had both completed their warm-up, they started to run along the coast towards East Beach. Lauren set the rhythm at her normal pace and Marc fell in beside her. They ran along in silence for the first mile or so and then Lauren started telling Marc about the history of the things they passed.

She told him about the controversy the dolphin fountain at the entrance to Stern's Wharf had caused when it had first been unveiled.

Residents in Santa Barbara were very concerned about the aesthetic beauty of the environment and everyone seemed to have a different idea regarding what was acceptable.

"Now that some time has passed since the dolphin fountain was installed it's considered a Santa Barbara landmark," Lauren laughed. "I've even seen photographs of the fountain on postcards sold to visiting tourists."

They continued to run along the paths that wound between the sand and the street and they enjoyed the smell of the sea air.

"Every Sunday there's an art show along the beach where we're running," Lauren told Marc as they continued on their way. "You might want to wander down here one afternoon."

Soon they were nearing the volleyball courts and Lauren was beginning to feel a little winded. She noticed that

Marc wasn't having any difficulty in keeping the rigorous pace she set for herself every day.

Their conversation stopped for a while as they continued running down the beach. It was a peaceful, sunny morning. The damp, salty sea air was very invigorating. They turned to the left and crossed the street to avoid traffic, entering the bird sanctuary located on the opposite side of the street from the beach. It was still early morning and the light shimmered off the large lagoon in front of them.

"It's beautiful here," Marc said in awe. "I had no idea this was here."

"This is one of the reasons I never get tired of running this path over and over again. There's always something new to see," Lauren replied. "If you'd like, one morning we can continue on and I can show you the Biltmore Hotel. It really is beautiful up through there as well." Lauren continued. "The Biltmore was built as a luxury resort years ago and is now one of the nicest hotels in the Santa Barbara area."

"Does this mean we're official running partners, Lauren?" Marc inquired.

Lauren realized she'd been presumptuous. It seemed natural to have him running next to her. "Well, didn't Leo assign me as your official tour guide while you're here in Santa Barbara?" she laughed.

"Are you sure Jim won't mind?" Marc asked.

"Well, Jim's not much of a runner. He doesn't understand why I run every day. I don't think he believes he's missing anything."

As they continued to run, it became more difficult to have a conversation and they ran the remaining distance in silence. When they reached the harbor they slowed to a walking pace to cool down from their exercise. Both of them were out of breath, but Lauren had to admit that Marc was in excellent condition. She was accustomed to running the length of the beach and back on a daily basis and Marc appeared to be less winded than she was. The day was beginning to warm and they both had become dehydrated during their trek.

"Do you want to get a drink?" Lauren asked. "I have water or juice at my apartment." Lauren got a little flustered at being so forward with Marc. "Actually, I meant to bring a water bottle with me and I forgot. I overslept," Lauren continued humbly.

Marc laughed. "Great minds forget alike," he said. "I had a water bottle by the door and then left my apartment without it."

"Well, come on then… my apartment is right around the corner," Lauren said, and the two of them started to walk up the street together.

They approached her apartment a few minutes later and Buster greeted Lauren as she approached.

"There you are, Buster!" she said as she scooped him up and gave him a kiss on the top of his head. "Where were you last night?" Lauren looked at Marc with a twinkle in her eye. "Mr. Marcus Harland, I would like to introduce you to Buster, my cat," she said formally and then laughed. "Buster scared me last night by not coming home. At least he seems to have survived without any additional scrapes," Lauren continued as she put Buster down and retrieved her keys from the flower box. As she started to unlock the door she noticed that Buster wandered over to Marc and was sniffing inquiringly. Marc seemed to pass inspection because Buster turned and wandered toward the back of the cottage without giving Marc another glance.

"Come on in and make yourself at home. I'll be right back. Do you want orange juice or water?"

"Water's fine, thanks."

Marc looked around the living room of Lauren's small apartment. There was a cream colored couch with several bright throw pillows and a glass coffee table with several magazines on top. An old, brick fireplace that had been painted white and two oversized chairs, one with an un-folded blanket strewn across it with a law book resting on the arm, were on either side. The room looked inviting and lived in. There were several paintings hanging on the white walls adding a splash of color along with a throw rug cov-ering a good portion of the parquet wood floor. Marc noticed that the decor was not expensive but well executed and made the small room appear cozy and inviting.

Lauren came back into the room carrying a bottle of mineral water and two glasses. She'd kicked off her run-ning shoes while she was gone and she hardly made a sound as she glided into the room. Marc turned and ob-served Lauren. *She's just like an angel,* he thought as she approached.

"Here you go... a cold, refreshing drink after a long, hot run," Lauren said as she poured the water and handed Marc one of the glasses. "I have to say, you were great today. I'm used to running that distance everyday, but it took me awhile to build up my stamina."

"I don't think I would have been able to live it down if I hadn't been able to keep up," laughed Marc. "Actually," he continued. "I really enjoy getting outside. It sure beats exercising in a crowded gym on a machine that doesn't go anywhere."

"I know what you mean," replied Lauren. She glanced at the clock on the mantle above the fireplace. "Oh no! Is it really eight fifteen?" she exclaimed. "I'm going to be late for work if I don't hurry...and so are you for that matter," she jokingly continued. "I'm sorry; I have to ask you to leave. Sorry to drink and run."

"Or run and drink. No problem, Lauren. I didn't realize how quickly the time went by," Marc replied as he put his glass down on the coffee table. "I have a meeting with Leo this morning so I need to hurry. I'll see you later," Marc said and then he was gone.

Lauren shut the door behind him and stood a minute before making her way towards her bedroom. What an unusual man. *He's not what I expected,* she thought to herself as she pulled off her running clothes and took a quick, cool shower. Marc was not the single-minded attorney focused solely on his career that she had pictured him to be.

Lauren did not have time to curl her hair so she pulled it back into a French braid and dressed in a navy suit-dress and heels. She picked out one of her scarves and pinned it across her shoulders, breaking the harsh line of the dress. Normally she didn't wear earrings because her long hair concealed them, but this morning she selected a pair of pearl earrings to frame her face.

She hurried out the door and headed for the office. She walked in just after nine o'clock, her normal starting hour. She put her purse in the bottom desk drawer and took a deep breath. *"Oh, where to begin?"* she thought as she jotted down a list of the items that needed to be completed that day.

She spent the majority of the morning going over the file notes she'd taken the last couple of days. She turned on her computer and typed up her analysis of the findings. She printed the final copy and placed the papers in a folder to discuss with Marc after he returned from his meeting with Leo. The trial date was getting closer and they needed to be sure they were prepared for all of the intricacies of the case.

Lauren reached into her desk drawer and pulled out her purse. She decided to take a break for lunch and she thought a walk outside would be refreshing.

As she walked out onto the main street she decided to walk a few blocks to a delicatessen. After ordering a sandwich, chips and drink she picked up a copy of the local weekly paper and waited for her order. When her food was ready, she decided to take it over to the courthouse lawn to eat in the sunken gardens.

The sun was shining, so she picked a cool, shady spot on a stone wall that surrounded the perimeter of the gardens. The greenery was well maintained and little brass plaques were posted alongside the plants in the garden indicating both the botanical and more common name of the particular variety. Lauren enjoyed strolling along the grounds reading about the various plants.

She sat on the wall, eating her lunch, watching the people around her. *Only in Santa Barbara would it be possible to play Frisbee on the grounds of the courthouse,* thought Lauren. She enjoyed the peaceful attitude that was prevalent in Santa Barbara. Lauren recognized several other employees of the local law firms relaxing in the gardens. Two people were throwing a Frisbee and several others were playing backgammon. The people in Santa Barbara were not afraid to work hard, but they tried to balance both the private and public side of their lives.

"Maybe I'm too worried about getting involved physically with Jim," Lauren thought to herself. The one brief relationship she had had while she was attending the university had become a distraction to her studies and it had scared her. Law school was just around the corner and she still hadn't decided if she was going to stay in Santa Barbara or go back home to Michigan. *Why is life always so complicated?* she asked herself.

Lauren looked at her watch and started to gather up the remains of her lunch. Her lunch hour seemed to fly by. She would have to stroll around reading about the garden another time. She already knew the majority of the plants and had memorized their botanical names, but she still found the walk enjoyable.

There was no sign of Marc or Leo when she returned to her office. She decided to continue working on the research for the case. It would be important for Marc to review the depositions carefully on his own even though Lauren had already highlighted significant areas. With Marc's experience he would be able to identify some of the finer elements of the case. It was Lauren's responsibility to assist with the research.

Lauren looked up when she heard a knock on the door.

"Leo wants to see you in his office right now, Lauren," Julie announced before she turned and walked away.

Although Lauren had a strong working relationship with Leo, being summoned to his office was not to be taken lightly. Lauren closed the file she was working on and headed down the hall.

The door to Leo's office was open and Lauren could see him talking on the phone, his back turned to the doorway. Lauren tapped on the open door to alert him of her presence and Leo turned and beckoned her into his office with a motion of his hand. Marc was nowhere to be seen.

"Sure, Stan... I agree, we should be able to tie up a settlement on this case within the next couple of days. Have your office send over the necessary paperwork and we'll take care of the rest," Leo continued with his call.

I wonder if the Consumer Energy case is being settled? Lauren thought to herself. It did not seem to be likely, not with Marc Harland on board. The firm was busy and always had several cases pending trial. *Well, I'll know soon enough,* Lauren thought as she waited patiently for Leo to finish his call.

"Good, good," Leo said into the phone in a satisfied manner. "I look forward to our golf game this weekend. Right now I've got to go, but let's make sure to have a celebratory drink on Saturday." Leo said goodbye and focused on Lauren.

"I met with Marc this morning..." Leo started and Lauren felt herself tense.

CHAPTER FOUR

Lauren sank deeper into the cool, luxurious waters of her bath and relaxed. After she'd left her office in the evening, Lauren had decided to take an exercise class at a local fitness club. The class combined aerobic and dance movements for a fun and exhilarating workout. The bath was soothing and refreshing after the hour long class.

Lauren groaned as she thought back to her meeting with the senior partner earlier that day.

"I met with Marc this morning and he told me he was very impressed with your knowledge and assistance," Leo had started. The compliment was unexpected.

"Thank you, Leo," Lauren had responded, somewhat at a loss for words.

"Marc told me he's found an apartment and has settled in very nicely," Leo went on. "I just want to make sure that Marc feels at home. Normally I wouldn't ask such a personal favor of you, Lauren, but since the two of you are working so closely together on the Consumer Energy case I think you should be the one to show Marc around. It's important to give him a good impression of our firm. After all, Marc Harland would make a very good addition. I don't want to give him any reason not to accept a full-time position with us once the trial is over."

"Yes, I know, Leo."

"Good, good," Leo continued, "As you know, Lily likes to throw a party every now and then and it seems like she invites as many people as possible." Lily was Leo's wife. "Personally I feel like scrooge and want to say 'bah hum-bug' to the whole thing. But Lily loves it and who am I to stand in her way," Leo said with a twinkle in his eye. The Whitmans had been married for almost forty years and Leo obviously adored his vivacious wife.

"Black-tie event, the whole nine yards," Leo continued. "I was hoping that you could attend and of course, Jim is invited as well." Leo picked up an envelope from the surface of his desk and handed it to Lauren. "I thought it would be a nice touch to hand-deliver the invitation. The party is three weeks from Saturday."

"Well...sure, Leo," Lauren had replied as she took the outstretched invitation. "I'll have to check if Jim will be able to join me, but I'll be sure to be there regardless. It sounds like it will be a marvelous party." *What is Jim going to say about this,* Lauren had wondered; however she did not know how to politely refuse Leo. Jim was not the type of man who enjoyed getting dressed up and going to a party.

"Oh, and Lauren..." Leo had broken through her concentration. "Marc will be attending the party as well. Maybe you could make sure he feels at home. I'll try to spend some time with him, but with this type of function I always get pulled in all different directions. Knowing you had your eye on him would sure help me out."

Lauren sank lower into the tub until the water level reached her chin. She had wanted to say no, but felt obligated to help Leo no matter how uncomfortable it made her.

The aromatic bath was soothing, but Lauren was still concerned about Jim. *I'll have to give him a call and find out if he's free for the party.* The bath water was beginning to cool and Lauren pulled the plug to the drain and stood up. She turned on the shower to rinse off and stepped out of the tub and dried her long, lithe frame. She strolled barefoot down the hallway of her apartment after putting on a thick, terry-cloth robe.

Lauren picked up the phone and dialed Jim's number. The phone rang several times as she waited for the answering machine to connect. After a few more unanswered rings, she finally hung up the phone. Apparently Jim did not set his machine before he left. *I wonder where he is?* Lauren thought. She had spoken to him earlier in the afternoon and he had indicated that he didn't have any special plans for that evening.

Lauren wandered around her home. She felt impatient and restless. She had wanted to tie up the loose ends with Jim regarding the party. Usually Lauren was a very patient person, but tonight she felt fidgety. She started to read one of the case books from the law library and found herself rereading the same paragraph without absorbing the information. She stopped trying to read and slapped the book shut.

Lauren finally decided to go to bed and try to sleep off her feelings of unease. She tossed and turned for several hours before falling into a light sleep that did not leave her feeling refreshed when she woke early the next morning.

Lauren made her way into the kitchen and poured herself a glass of orange juice. She hadn't seen Marc at the office during the previous day and she didn't know if he was planning on joining her on her morning run or not. She decided to walk down to the harbor and start her stretching. If Marc didn't arrive within fifteen minutes she would start the run by herself.

When she reached the harbor she looked around for Marc and felt a twinge of disappointment when she didn't see him. She started doing her warm-up stretching. She subconsciously moved slowly, delaying the onset of her run.

The sun cast an early morning ray of light across the water causing it to glisten and sparkle. There was a slight morning breeze that rippled the sails on the boats in the harbor. Most of the sails were lowered and tied to the boat booms, but several morning boaters were beginning to raise their sails in preparation for their morning departure.

Lauren, being from the Midwest, was fascinated by the sailboats, both large and small. She watched one of the boats sail into the harbor, preparing to dock. *That's unusual,* she thought. *Most boats are leaving early in the morning, not arriving.* As the boat glided into an empty slip and stopped, Lauren watched the strong powerful arms of the man aboard as he lowered the sails and secured them to the boom of the boat. It caught her by surprise when she realized that the sailor was Marc Harland.

Lauren made her way down the wooden dock. "Good morning!" she called out to get Marc's attention.

"Hey, good morning. I wasn't sure if I was going to get back in time to meet you to run. The wind shifted on me and it took me a little longer to get back than I anticipated," Marc responded.

Lauren looked at the boat. It was a beautiful, sleek craft painted white with maroon striping. The stern of the boat was painted with the name "My Only Love," with "San Francisco, California" underneath. It wasn't an exceptionally large boat and could easily be maneuvered by one person. Lauren could see steps leading downwards into the hull of the boat. There were several floats and life jackets on the deck of the boat. Lauren could also see a wetsuit and an oxygen tank.

Lauren looked closer at Marc and realized that his hair was slightly damp and, even though he was currently dressed in a t-shirt and shorts, along with deck shoes, she assumed he'd been diving earlier that morning.

"The water is great here. It's a lot warmer than San Francisco, that's for sure," Marc said, smiling as he jumped from the boat onto the dock and securely tied the boat to the slip. Jumping back aboard the boat, he called over his shoulder, "Just give me a second to store these things down below and I'll be ready to go."

Marc quickly gathered up the items on boat deck and went down the steps into the hull of the boat. He soon reappeared and shut a door, closing off the stairs. He pulled keys out of the pocket of his shorts and locked the doors and turned toward Lauren. "All set."

Marc jumped back onto the deck and Lauren realized he had changed from his topsiders into a pair of running shoes. He was also carrying a bottle of water in a net bag with a long strap. Once he was on the dock he slung the strap over his shoulder, diagonally across his chest.

"How did you manage to get a slip in Santa Barbara? It's almost impossible from what I've heard."

Marc laughed. "Well, I had a good bargaining chip. I've had a slip in San Francisco for a while which is another sought after commodity. A friend of mine who lives in Santa Barbara was interested in trading places for the three months that I'm here. It actually worked out very well for both of us."

Lauren and Marc walked the length of the pier towards the grassy area where they had stretched the morning before. Even though Lauren had already performed her warm-up exercises, she'd felt her muscles stiffen while standing still on the dock. The two of them started to stretch.

"How about heading out by the Biltmore today?" Marc asked.

"Unfortunately, I have to get into the office early today. I don't think I have time. You can continue on if you would like, but I'll have to turn back at the bird sanctuary."

"That's alright, I'll complete the run with you. We can always go up to the Biltmore another day."

Lauren felt a sense of exhilaration. The subconscious fear she had had earlier about him not showing up disappeared leaving her feeling free and light-spirited. She started to run, avoiding a closer examination of her feelings.

They ran together in silence for the first portion of the path. The water bottle that was hung diagonally across Marc's body made a gentle, sloshing sound that blended with the waves pounding against the shore. Occasionally a sea gull squawk could be heard, the sound carrying in the early morning breeze from off the water. The smell of salt water filled their nostrils and left them feeling energized.

"Are you all settled in your apartment?" Lauren asked as they started to wind their way along the path.

"Yeah, it didn't take too long. I only brought the things that I would need for the time I'm here." Lauren was reminded that Marc viewed his stay in Santa Barbara as a temporary one. *Leo is going to be very disappointed,* Lauren thought. She did not want to think about how she was going to feel when Marc left Santa Barbara.

They ran the majority of the way in silence, only speaking occasionally when Lauren pointed out various birds and vegetation along the way.

"Let me know if I'm boring you," said Lauren.

"Not at all, you're certainly very knowledgeable. You know a lot more than I do."

Lauren smiled. "I started trying to identify the birds and plants along the way to make the run a little different every time. I bought several books on the subject when I couldn't figure out some of the species I found," she continued. "Soon I was able to identify most of the birds and plants. There are a few times now that I see a bird I haven't seen before and need to look it up, but I used to be looking up several a day!"

Marc laughed. "You seem very determined with your research both in and out of the office."

Lauren was surprised how disappointed she felt by his statement. Although she felt complimented, his remark also made her feel he only saw her as a competent paralegal.

The several meals that they'd shared and their runs in the morning had made Lauren hope for more of a friendship with Marc.

What had she been thinking? She had to keep reminding herself that Marc would be leaving soon. *He's not going to want to be bothered with me after he's gone. All the more reason for me to keep my distance from Marc Harland,* she thought to herself.

They had circled around and were making their way back to the harbor. They both slowed to a walking pace to cool off from their run. Marc removed the water bottle and handed it to Lauren and she drank from it gratefully. She handed it back and Marc's hand brushed hers in the transfer. His touch was electric and Lauren pulled back, reminding herself to keep her distance. *He does have nice, strong hands though,* Lauren thought.

"Well, I have to hurry if I'm going to make it into the office on time," Lauren said as she turned toward the street leading to her apartment. "I'll see you later."

"Bye, Lauren," Marc replied and then added "Good run. Tomorrow same place and time?"

"Sure," Lauren threw over her shoulder and hurried away. "How am I going to keep my distance from this man when Leo has asked me to play baby sitter?" Lauren muttered to herself. "He certainly seems like a big boy capable of taking care of himself," She added to herself as she fiddled with the key and unlocked her apartment.

Lauren and Marc established a daily running routine during the next couple of days. They met by the harbor then stretched and ran the length of East Beach and back. They'd decided that the Biltmore run would be easier on a Saturday or Sunday morning when there were no time constraints.

They were beginning to establish a routine at the office as well. Marc joined Lauren for part of the day in the law library and they reviewed her findings together. Marc was very appreciative and helpful. On several occasions, he pointed her in a direction she hadn't considered.

Lauren allowed herself the luxury of sleeping later on the weekend and it was eight-thirty when her alarm sounded. She had arranged to meet Marc at nine. After she dressed, she made her way into the kitchen and poured herself a small glass of juice. She was careful not to drink too much because she didn't want to get a cramp during her run.

The morning was a typical, sunny day in Santa Barbara. A few light, cumulus clouds were visible in the sky. Lauren noticed the blue sky and clouds as she went outside, her keys in hand to lock her front door. As she started to insert the key, she could hear her phone start to ring inside. She quickly reopened the door and hurried to answer the phone before her answering machine picked up.

"Hello," Lauren said breathlessly into the phone.

"Promise me you'll sound like that when I see you next?" asked Jim. Lauren could feel herself cringe.

"I was outside and had to run for the phone," Lauren said, trying to keep the irritation out of her voice. "I'm on my way out to meet Marc for our morning run," she continued. "Can I call you later?"

"What is it about that guy? I thought you liked to run by yourself."

"Generally, I do, but Leo has asked me to help Marc feel at home while he's here," Lauren answered and then added, "I told you about that, Jim. It's nothing, really. Besides, I find I enjoy his company. He gives me a lot of encouragement."

"Well, I don't like it," Jim said curtly. "Anyway, I just called to find out if we're getting together tonight?"

Lauren felt perplexed. Of course they were going out; he had called yesterday to ask the same question. Something was nagging at Lauren and she could not put her finger on it.

"Well, sure Jim, of course."

"Fine Lauren. I'll pick you up at eight."

Lauren replaced the receiver of the phone on the cradle and shook her head. "I must be going crazy..." she mumbled as she retraced her steps to the front door. *Actually, I think Jim is the one who's crazy calling twice to confirm,* she thought to herself as she locked the front door. She glanced at her watch after she put the keys in the flower box. *Five minutes past nine. Where did all my free time go? Now I'm late,* she thought as she hurried toward the beach.

Lauren apologized to Marc when she arrived. She had been able to watch him for a while before she was within speaking distance. *I don't believe he only runs and sails a boat...No one could be that lucky,* Lauren thought. She felt that she was lucky to an extent as well because running enabled her to eat a lot of the food she liked, but she still needed to be sensible and not over-indulge. During the several meals that she had shared with Marc she hadn't noticed him skimping on anything at all.

"Ready for a Saturday morning extra?" Marc asked with a twinkle in his eye.

"What?"

"The extra portion of our run," Marc explained. "Don't tell me you forgot about running down past the Biltmore?"

"No, no..." Lauren was disturbed by Jim's call and she wasn't thinking about the run. "I'm sorry, my mind must have been somewhere else... I'll be done stretching in a minute."

Marc looked puzzled. During the last week he felt he was beginning to understand the woman in front of him. Somehow looking at her now, like he had at other times during the week, she didn't strike him as a woman in love. But he'd met Jim. He hadn't been very impressed with the man, but Lauren and Jim certainly appeared to be together.

"Take your time. Remember, on the weekends we have all the time we need." Lauren finished her warm-up and within a few minutes they were off and running.

The first portion of their run was familiar and routine. However, instead of circling the sanctuary they crossed the street and ran along the perimeter where there was a path for bikes and pedestrians. Soon they crossed back to the side they had started from to take a side road that led to the hotel. A low, stone wall, along with heavy traffic, made it nearly impossible to remain on the same side of the road for the entire run.

The Biltmore was a beautiful and impressive old hotel dating back to the late nineteen twenties. The hotel was built along the coast and the waves crashing against the shore had a soothing and relaxing rhythm. At first Lauren and Marc had run inland and the road toward the Biltmore led them back along the coastline. Lauren was surprised to notice the difference that the cool breeze coming off of the ocean made.

"Do you have much planned for the weekend, Marc?"

"I'm going to go into the office for a little while this morning, but tomorrow I'm planning on taking the boat out. I thought I might try to make it out to one of the Channel Islands and back."

"That sounds wonderfully relaxing," Lauren responded.

"Hey, I've got a great idea...Why don't you join me?" Marc said as they slowed to cool off.

"I don't know...It certainly was not my intention to coerce you into an invitation," Lauren replied.

"I wouldn't have asked unless I wanted you to come with me, Lauren."

"Well, I'll need to talk to Jim before I can commit to anything."

"Bring him along. There's room enough for all of us." Marc was surprised at how much the thought of the other man made him bristle. He hadn't been impressed with Jim during dinner the other night and wondered what attracted Lauren to him.

"How about if I call you later this afternoon and let you know." Lauren loved the thought of sailing on the ocean. She had wondered many times what it would be like, but she had never afforded the luxury. The thought of going out with Marc on his boat was exciting, but she still felt a need to check with Jim first.

Since the beginning of the week, Lauren had been feeling the strain in her relationship with Jim. He'd been applying pressure that had made her feel uncomfortable, even after the understanding they had reached several weeks earlier.

"That's fine. I'm planning on going anyway, so you won't be preventing me from taking the trip," Marc answered. "Hey, do you want to go into the cafe over there and get something to drink?" Marc asked as they slowed to a walking pace.

Cabrillo Boulevard, which wound along the coastline, was filled with a variety of hotels and restaurants. "I've got the bottled water, but it's Saturday, we should make this a complete outing," Marc continued as he steered Lauren towards the restaurant entrance.

"A nice, iced drink does sound good right about now," Lauren laughed. "And it doesn't seem like I have much of a choice."

Marc mimicked a stricken look on his face. "Lauren, my dear, you always have a choice. As an attorney I do hope I know the law." The look on Marc's face made Lauren laugh and she could feel her heart skip a beat with the endearment.

They slid into a nearby booth and Marc picked up two of the plastic encased menus and flourished the menu open for Lauren. "Madam..." he said with an exaggerated French accent.

"Marrying me off so quickly..." Lauren responded with a laugh that caught in her throat as Marc's expression changed.

"No, of course not. Remember, you always have a choice." He looked at her closely and Lauren felt flustered and clumsy as she reached to take a sip from the glass of water in front of her.

Marc looked at the menu. "I don't know about you, but I'm starving. Let's order a big breakfast."

The return of Marc's lighthearted attitude made Lauren relax a little. "If I keep eating the way I have this past week, I'll have more than just a big breakfast, I'll have a big body as well."

Marc glanced appreciatively towards Lauren's curves. "Well, you seem perfect the way you are now. Whatever you've been doing seems to be working just fine." As the waitress appeared he looked at Lauren. "Ready?"

After they ordered they were silent for a minute. Lauren was still flustered by Marc's compliments and she busied herself putting the menus back into the metal slot at the end of their booth.

Lauren and Marc enjoyed a wonderful meal of scrambled eggs, bacon and toast with homemade pan fried potatoes with onions and peppers. Marc proved to be witty and a pleasant breakfast companion. He was relaxed and comfortable to be with and his attitude made Lauren respond openly to him.

She learned that Marc's parents were retired and living up the coast in Carmel. His father had been an air force pilot and Marc had spent a lot of his childhood traveling around the United States. His younger sister, Jenny, worked as a flight attendant for a commercial airline.

Lauren told Marc about her parents who lived in Michigan. She was an only child. Her father owned a small grocery store and her mother worked as a secretary for a local doctor.

They laughed together as Marc shared accounts of his younger sister's antics. As Lauren listened, she thought it must be wonderful to have someone to grow up with. Marc's stories confirmed a decision Lauren had made earlier in her life. A decision that she would have at least two children if she ever got married. *I bet Marc would be an excel-*

lent father, Lauren thought wistfully. As she realized where her thoughts had taken her, she tried to strengthen her resolve to keep her distance from Marc Harland. He'd been very clear during their first lunch together that when the case was over he would be gone.

Marc was intrigued with the beautiful woman who sat across from him. Lauren Evans was intelligent, relaxed and enjoyable to be with. He didn't know how long it had been since he had laughed so much.

Marc found himself wondering what it would be like to touch her smooth, peach-colored skin and feel her full lips brush against his own. The direction of his thoughts caught Marc off-guard. *Be careful, buddy,* he told himself. *You have to work with this woman for the next several months.* Marc tried to shake the mental images of Lauren from his mind as he finished eating his eggs and potatoes.

CHAPTER FIVE

The next several weeks passed quickly for Lauren. The trial date was getting closer and the last minute details of the case took the majority of her time.

Lauren had gone out with Jim after her Saturday run with Marc and several times since, but their relationship was strained. Jim seemed distracted the majority of the time and self-absorbed. Lauren was starting to wonder if it was a n e w trait or a side of Jim's personality that she had not consciously acknowledged.

Lauren had declined Marc's offer to go sailing after discussing the outing with Jim. He'd reacted badly to the prospect of spending the afternoon on a boat with Marcus Harland and had used the opportunity to criticize the attorney. "There he goes again, flaunting his money," Jim had growled.

Lauren had cringed at Jim's reaction. She found she enjoyed spending time with Marc. Because of Jim's reaction, she felt it was better to keep the two men apart. Marc had always been a perfect gentleman, but Lauren was worried about Jim's behavior.

If Leo had not asked Lauren to be a representative of the firm she might not have felt as concerned, but considering the circumstances, she would not like word getting back to Leo if Jim were to misbehave. Lately, Lauren felt that Jim was no longer predictable, almost like a loose cannon waiting to be set off.

Lauren was sitting in her office, reviewing her case notes when there was a light tap on the door. She looked up to see Marc standing in the doorway. Her breath caught in her throat at the sight of him. He was wearing a dark, navy suit but had removed the jacket to reveal a crisp white shirt and paisley suspenders. The sleeves of his shirt were turned up to reveal his strong, toned arms. His dark hair looked perfect and the dark tan, from daily running and occasional sailing, made his blue eyes and white teeth sparkle.

"Good run this morning," He started. They had been running every morning for the last few weeks. "I wanted to let you know that Leo needs me to work out a couple of details in Los Angeles next week, so I won't be able to run with you in the morning."

"Oh... fine," Lauren had replied, not willing to examine her sudden feelings of regret. Marc sensed her change in emotion and continued, "I'll be able to run with you tomorrow, but I'm leaving on Sunday morning. With Leo and Lily's party tomorrow night, it's going to be a late night. I don't think I'll have time to go running on Sunday before I have to leave for Los Angeles."

"No problem," Lauren responded calmly. "Are you looking forward to the Whitman's party?"

"Sure, from what little I know of Lily Whitman, it sounds extravagant. Promise me a dance, will you?" It was more of a statement than a question and Marc turned to leave. "I've got a meeting with Leo, but I'll see you later."

The Whitman's party was only a day away. It seemed like yesterday that Leo had extended the invitation.

Lauren looked at her watch and was surprised to find that it was almost five o'clock. She needed to get a few items to be prepared for the party the next night. It shouldn't take her long to pick up hair clips and special hosiery with a jeweled design she had seen in the store several days earlier but had not been able to buy at the time. There was also a pair of black satin shoes that she had debated about purchasing and she had finally decided to give in and splurge. She had bought a dress the previous weekend and had planned on wearing a pair of black pumps she normally wore to the office but when she had put the two together it didn't create the desired effect.

Jim had agreed to go to the party with Lauren somewhat begrudgingly. Since agreeing to go he had complained several times about renting a tuxedo and Lauren had finally snapped at him telling him to either go or not go to the party but to stop trying to make her feel guilty about it. Her spark of anger had surprised her, but Jim's attitude was wearing her nerves thin. After her declaration, Jim sheepishly apologized and did not complain again. Lauren was feeling uncomfortable and nervous about the upcoming evening and Jim's attitude put a damper on her feelings of expectation and excitement.

Saturday passed quickly. Lauren had met Marc in the morning for their run, but he had needed to spend time in the office and didn't have the additional time with Lauren as he'd had during their previous Saturday morning runs to venture towards the Biltmore.

It was almost eight-thirty in the evening when Lauren clipped large faux jewels to her earlobes and nervously straightened her dress. *Jim should be arriving any minute,* she thought as she looked into the mirror one last time to evaluate her appearance.

She'd pulled her auburn hair up into a French twist, leaving several loose tendrils curling down around her face. With her hair swept up, the jeweled earrings caught the light and sparkled, lighting her whole face. The dress she'd chosen was sleek and black with a basic design that was simple but extremely elegant. It was cut long, but had a high slit on the one side, revealing glimpses of her long, slender legs as she moved. The nylons and shoes rounded out her appearance, with just enough sparkle to the hosiery to accent the dress.

Jim knocked on the door shortly after Lauren's final assessment and she opened the door to find him looking uncomfortable in his rented tuxedo. The tuxedo looked elegant, but somehow on Jim, it didn't have any style. Lauren collected a small satin purse that complemented her new shoes and they headed out to Jim's car.

The cocktail party was well under way by the time Lauren and Jim pulled up to the front door where a young man in a short valet jacket opened the door for Lauren and replaced Jim at the wheel to park the car.

The Whitman's home was beautiful, nestled along the shore in Montecito, an exclusive community located south of Santa Barbara. The front entrance had two large glass doors that led into the foyer. Beyond the foyer was another set of glass doors. The end result was an unblocked view from the front driveway through the house to the ocean beyond.

Lauren and Jim entered the house and were immediately greeted by Lily Whitman, a beautiful woman in her sixties with short, white hair cut in an elegant style.

"Lauren! Jim! I'm so glad the two of you could make it. The bar is down that way if you'd like a mixed drink or something a little softer. There's also a beer and wine bar set up in the back by the pool if that's more to your liking."

"Hello, Lily," Lauren said warmly, grasping the outstretched hands of the other woman. "It really looks like you've outdone yourself again." The house was decorated with large arrangements of fresh flowers, along with garlands and ribbons around the tabletops and mantle. The sound of jazz music was coming from one direction and mingled with the sounds of voices and laughter coming from the living room below.

Lauren and Jim made their way down the several steps that led into the large living room below. A grand piano was located to the left near several French doors. A fireplace with a large mantle and hearth were located directly in front of Lauren as she moved into the room. To the right was an alcove that led into the family room. Several people were lounging on the overstuffed chairs and couch located around the fireplace and many others were standing around the bar talking in small groups.

"I'm getting a drink," Jim said and walked off, leaving Lauren to follow behind. After getting a scotch for himself, he turned to Lauren. "What do you want?" he asked impatiently.

After getting Lauren a drink of cranberry juice mixed with orange juice, they made their way towards the back of the house. They walked out onto the back patio and the party transformed into a twinkling festival of lights. Little white lights had been strung in the trees and they sparkled in the cool evening air.

"How magical!" Lauren gasped. The lights shimmered, and reflected in the water of the pool. The sound from the jazz band filtered outside and seemed to float out onto the ocean.

Lauren saw Leo standing off to one side, talking to several of his guests. "I'm going to say hello to Leo. Do you want to tag along?" Lauren asked Jim.

"No, I'm going to get another drink," Jim replied. Lauren noticed that he'd already finished his scotch and was heading towards the bar.

Lauren was worried about Jim's recent drinking. It seemed out of character for him, but she was beginning to realize how little she knew about him. It occurred to her that she talked more openly and freely with Marc than she ever had with Jim during the entire time they had dated.

Left on her own, Lauren made her way over towards Leo. When he saw her approaching he excused himself from the group he was with and headed towards her with his arms outstretched. "Lauren, my you do look lovely this evening. Are you having a good time?"

"Jim and I only just arrived, but the party looks wonderful. I'm just beginning to explore."

"Good, good. There's a whole buffet set up in the dining room and Lily had me arrange for a dance floor to be installed over the carpet in the family room."

"I haven't been there yet, but it sounds like fun."

"I used to be a real hoofer in my day. You'll have to save a dance for me."

Lauren laughed. "I'm sure I'll be the one trying to keep up, Leo. Consider yourself on my dance card."

"Good, good. I haven't seen Marc yet, but I'm sure he'll be here soon. It's comforting to know you'll have your eye on him. I always feel pulled in so many directions at this type of thing," Leo said. "Like now," he continued as he waved to someone across from them. "I've got to go, but I'll find you later. I don't want to miss out on my dance."

Lauren found herself standing alone and decided to make a tour of the rest of the house. The buffet was extravagant with every type of food imaginable. She picked up a stuffed mushroom and nibbled it absentmindedly as she made her way to the dance floor.

It was still early and only a few couples had ventured onto the floor. Most of the guests were out by the pool or in the living room. The party would probably be in full swing within an hour.

Lauren stopped to talk to several people from the office, but for the most part, the party consisted of people she didn't know.

She decided to make her way back to the living room to find Jim. As she started down the stairs, she gasped as she saw Marc. She was stunned by the appearance of him in formal attire. After spending so much time with him in the office or running, the transformation took her breath away. The tuxedo he was wearing fit him perfectly, his broad shoulders filling every inch of the jacket. He looked powerful and impressive as he reached for the glass the bartender extended towards him.

As he turned away from the bar, he saw Lauren frozen on the step and his dark blue eyes embraced her from across the room. Lauren couldn't break her gaze away from him and their eyes locked for what seemed like forever. Marc's expression reflected something Lauren couldn't quite discern.

Marc was the first to move, coming towards her to take her elbow and guide her into the room. "You look stunning," he said quietly into her ear. Lauren's heart skipped a beat and she felt like she floated into the room. The other guests seemed to part to either side to allow them to pass.

"Have you been here long?" Lauren asked, somewhat at a loss for words. She was caught off guard by the connection they'd made from across the room and she wondered if he'd felt the same reaction. She tried to push the significance of their magnetism from her mind.

"I just arrived," Marc answered as they made their way towards the grand piano. The jazz band was located in the family room and wasn't utilizing the beautiful instrument. "Have a seat; it appears the only one left in the room is the piano bench." Lauren glanced around and observed the huddled groups of people occupying the other pieces of furniture in the room. The two of them seem isolated, tucked away in the corner.

"Do you play?" Lauren asked.

"Not really. My mother always wanted me to play, but with my father moving the family from one military base to another, I think my mother felt she spent more time trying to find me a teacher than I spent actually playing."

Lauren noticed that Marc always spoke of his family with love and affection. *His family must be very special to him,* she thought to herself as her fingers lightly stroked the top of the ivory keys.

"I've always wanted to play, but never had the opportunity," Lauren replied wistfully. "Maybe I'll be able to learn sometime. Have you seen Leo? He mentioned you earlier this evening."

"Good comments, I hope," answered Marc with a twinkle in his eyes.

"Actually, he wanted me to keep an eye on you and make sure that you have a good time," answered Lauren truthfully.

"You've done your job so far. Want to make my night truly enjoyable by sharing a dance with me?"

"Well...I don't know," Lauren replied playfully. "My dance card seems pretty full, but I guess I can squeeze you in." Together they stood up and headed for the dance floor.

Several couples were already dancing and a few more were heading towards the floor, but they had the majority of the dance floor to themselves. Marc gathered Lauren up into his arms and took full advantage of the large floor. His strong, powerful arms guided her around the room and Lauren had the sensation of floating again for the second time that evening.

They complemented each other perfectly. They had started the dance with a courteous space between them, but as they found the rhythm of the music, their bodies came closer together, swaying in time to the melody. Lauren could feel Marc's powerful legs as he propelled her across the floor. She pressed her cheek against his chest to stabilize herself, her knees suddenly feeling weak as she came into closer contact with Marc. The song started to fade away as she became enveloped within his grasp. No one else seemed to exist outside of the circle of their arms.

Marc let out a groan and Lauren thought it felt like his lips brushed the top of her head. She pulled her cheek away from his chest and looked up at him. His eyes seemed darker than before and she looked expectantly up into his gaze.

His kiss seemed like a natural progression to their dancing. His lips covered hers in a gentle, teasing way which quickly became harder and more urgent in their need. Lauren could feel her body respond and she arched against him and returned his kiss without thinking.

Suddenly Marc pulled back and pushed her to arm's length. "I'm sorry Lauren; I don't usually make a habit of moving in on another man's date."

Jim! Lauren hadn't thought about him since she'd met up with Marc and she certainly hadn't thought about him during their kiss. Marc's kiss was confident, sensual and removed all sense of reason and logic from Lauren's mind. The kisses she shared with Jim were downright tame by comparison.

Lauren was stunned. *What is happening to me?*, she thought to herself. Marc was propelling her off the dance floor and dismissed himself abruptly. "Forgive me, I overstepped the boundaries." He turned and walked away.

How could she explain to Marc that she was able to date whomever she pleased? She'd lost her opportunity on the dance floor and she was still feeling a little dazed. Her lips still tingled from the contact of Marc's lips and there was a lingering current she felt internally.

The remainder of the party passed slowly. She'd decided to find Jim and had found him laughing and joking with Sylvia Lewis. *Of course*, Lauren thought, *Marc obviously came to the party with Sylvia.* The thought made her feel uncomfortable.

Shortly after exchanging pleasantries with Sylvia, Lauren looked at Jim and could tell he'd been drinking a fair amount. The only positive result was that he seemed to be having a fairly good time. Lauren had hoped to make an early departure from the party, but now that Sylvia had showed up and Jim seemed to be having a good time, she couldn't easily suggest that they leave.

Lauren saw Marc approaching the three of them and her mind replayed the kiss they had shared. She could see that he'd regained his composure and Marc greeted all three of them individually when he approached.

After discussing the party briefly and complementing the Whitmans for a well-executed event, Marc turned to Sylvia. "Would you like to dance?" he asked. Sylvia coyly looked up at Marc and purred her acceptance. As they turned towards the dance area, Marc looked at Jim. "You don't mind do you?" he asked and then guided the blond to the dance floor.

Jim looked sheepishly back at Marc and Lauren wondered why Marc had asked for Jim's permission to dance with Sylvia. Lauren dismissed Marc's request from her mind, feeling that the question was posed more out of courtesy considering that Jim and Sylvia were in the middle of a conversation.

Lauren watched the two move away towards the dance floor with a twinge of regret. Marc was an excellent dancer and with the recent kiss they had shared, it was apparent that Marc was going to be keeping his distance from her in the future. Lauren thought it was ironic, considering she'd been spending the last few weeks trying not to get too close to Marc Harland while at the same time Leo had done nothing except push the two of them together.

Lauren turned to Jim in time to see him swallow the last of his current drink. It was going to be a long night. "Would you like to dance, Jim?" Lauren asked, although she was not sure how well he would be able to maneuver the dance floor. Considering the time they'd been apart, it was likely that he had consumed a considerable amount of alcohol.

"Sure, hon," he slurred as they made their way towards the dance floor, following Marc and Sylvia.

The music was slow as Jim took Lauren into his arms and led her around the floor. Although his step was slightly offbeat, he was able to keep pace with the music without too much difficulty. Lauren let out a sigh of relief. Hopefully Jim would be sober enough to drive her back to her apartment.

The night was still young and Lauren began to review her options for getting home. Maybe Jim would give her his car keys and let her drive. Lauren shook her head. It seemed unlikely that Jim would relinquish his keys in front of the other guests. She also didn't relish the idea of having a repeat performance of Jim's behavior of several weeks ago.

Lauren continued to ponder her alternatives. She could always call them a cab, but then they would have to return the next day to retrieve Jim's car. Lauren was concerned about the message that would send to Leo. She was still a junior member of the firm and she felt a sense of responsibility to act maturely and professionally. Although leaving the car to avoid driving intoxicated was admirable,

Jim should never have had so much to drink. Lauren began to look around her and decided that Jim was not alone. Several other guests appeared equally intoxicated. Lauren tried to relax. *Well, at least it won't be as unsettling to come by in the morning to pick up Jim's car,* she thought to herself. Recognizing that Jim was not the only intoxicated person at the party made Lauren feel a little more comfortable about asking her host if she could leave Jim's car and retrieve it in the morning.

The pace of the music began to heighten and Jim increased his dancing speed. Lauren had a difficult time keeping up with him because his movements were erratic from the alcohol.

"Jim, I would like to sit down," Lauren started, but Jim cut her off.

"This is fun...I haven't danced like this for a while. Come on, honey...just one more song," was his slurred response.

Lauren agreed, praying that the song would end quickly. Jim took her nod of agreement as the signal to incorporate a wilder step and with his arm tightly around her waist, Lauren felt trapped.

"Jim, do you mind if I cut in?" a voice said behind her and Lauren exhaled a sigh of relief as Jim let go of her waist and stepped back to allow Leo Whitman to take over the dance.

"Your young man seems to have had a little bit too much to drink tonight, Lauren," Leo said. "It looked like you could do with an interruption. I hope you don't mind."

"Was it that obvious?" Lauren laughed and then continued. "I'm sorry, Leo. Normally Jim doesn't drink but lately..."

"Lauren, it's not my place to interfere, but you both are more than welcome to spend the night here. It really doesn't look like he should be driving. Consider that an open invitation, but for now, just put it out of your mind and let's enjoy our dance."

Leo moved with a grace and style developed over many years of dancing. Lauren didn't need to concentrate as she was whisked away. Dancing with Jim had required her full attention and now, dancing with Leo, Lauren was able to look around her and observe the other couples on the dance floor. Marc was located across the room, dancing with Lily Whitman and several other couples glided in between them.

"So, have you had much time to spend with Marc this evening or has that man of yours occupied all your time."

Lauren could feel her face flush, remembering the kiss that she had shared with Marc. Lauren was sure that was not the type of attention Leo had expected her to give Marc. Luckily there hadn't been a lot of people around earlier and Lauren hoped that the kiss had gone by unnoticed.

"I saw Marc briefly. Don't worry; I'll try to spend a little more time with him before the night is over," Lauren replied. She suddenly felt nervous. How was she going to accomplish that, she wondered. Marc was obviously with Sylvia and after he'd bolted earlier, Lauren was sure that the last place Marc Harland would want to be was with her.

"Good, good. Actually, I think I see a perfect way right now," and without warning, Leo waltzed Lauren across the floor.

"Marc, you don't mind if I dance with my wife, do you?" Leo said. "And besides, I'm offering you a substitute dance partner, if she's willing."

"Certainly, Leo." Marc stepped back and turned toward Lily. "It was enjoyable dancing with you, Lily." Lauren watched the older couple glide away from them.

"Well, are you willing?" Marc said. "Or, of course, we can always sit this one out."

"I...I don't mind dancing," Lauren replied and she hoped she would be able to explain everything to Marc while she had his full attention.

Lauren slipped into his arms and a feeling of coming home washed over her. Any thoughts of explaining her relationship with Jim to Marc vanished as she melted against his strong, muscular chest. The music that had been moving at a fast tempo had slowed while she had been dancing with Leo and the band continued with more of the same slow, rhythmic music.

They didn't speak as they moved around the dance floor. Lauren was aware of his strong arms around her. Before, when Jim had been holding her, she'd felt trapped, but now, with Marc's arms around her, she felt protected.

The melodic song they'd been dancing to ended and it took Lauren a minute to realize that Marc had stopped dancing and was pulling away from her.

"Thank you for the dance, Lauren. If you'll excuse me..." and Lauren watched him move away. Why hadn't she taken the time to explain her relationship with Jim and clear up their previous misunderstanding?

Lauren found Jim near the bar and they mingled with some of the other guests. The Whitmans had a variety of friends and Lauren tried to put Marc out of her mind and focus on the couple that she and Jim were talking to. The strain of the evening was beginning to catch up with Lauren and she felt as if a weight had settled upon her shoulders. After the couple had moved on towards the buffet, Lauren turned to Jim. "I'd like to go, it's getting late."

"Fine, I can hardly wait to get out of this monkey suit," Jim responded, fidgeting in his tuxedo. "Maybe I can take it off at your place..."

It was obvious that Jim had had too much to drink. "Jim I think we should get a cab. You really shouldn't drive your car..."

"I feel fine. Actually, I feel better than fine. Come, on Lauren, let's go to your place." Jim reached out to grab her and tried to kiss her neck.

Lauren tried to push him away. "Jim! Stop it!"

"Oh, I like it when you get feisty like this," Jim responded without loosening his grip.

Lauren could feel herself being propelled backwards, away from Jim and it caught her by surprise to see Marc separating the two of them.

"Well, hello there..." Marc said, enunciating each word slowly and carefully. "Jim, my man, it does appear that you have had too much to drink."

Jim's attitude changed dramatically, sneering in respond to Marc. "It really is none of your damn business, is it, Harland?"

"It is my business when it involves my paralegal." Marc turned to Lauren and held out his arm. "If you would like, I can drive you home." Lauren, in a daze took his arm. Marc turned back towards Jim, "The Whitmans have offered you a room to sleep it off. I suggest you take it... now, if you will excuse us."

Marc led Lauren out to the entrance and handed the valet his parking voucher. They stood there silently as the valet went to retrieve Marc's car.

"Thank you for rescuing me. I'm sorry, but Jim tends to overindulge sometimes."

"You shouldn't have to apologize for him, Lauren."

"Marc, I can get a cab. You really don't have to take me home."

The valet pulled up in a convertible Porsche and came around to open the door for Lauren. "I don't mind taking you home, Lauren, and you would have to wait a long time for a cab to make it out here. Get into the car."

Lauren slid into the leather seat offered her and she watched Marc walk over to the driver side of the car, tip the valet and slide in beside her.

Marc turned and leaned towards her. Lauren could smell the familiar scent of his aftershave as he reached across her and retrieved the seat belt and clipped it into place. "I hope you don't mind, but I like my passengers to be safe."

Lauren tried to laugh. "Is there something I should know about your driving? Maybe I would have been safer with Jim after all."

"I drive fine. It's other drivers like Jim that I'm concerned about." Marc fastened his own belt, put the car into gear and eased out of the driveway.

Lauren nestled into the seat of the car and looked up at the starry sky above her. The breeze was cool but not cold and it loosened several wisps of her hair. She had felt tired before, but sitting next to Marc with the stars above them she began to feel revitalized.

They drove along in silence for the first mile before Lauren started a conversation.

"Thank you for the ride. I wasn't sure how I was going to get home when I saw how much Jim was drinking."

"It's alright... but..."

"But what?" Lauren prompted.

"Nothing." Marc exited off the freeway and maneuvered the turns by the bird sanctuary with ease. As they started driving along the stretch of beach on Cabrillo Boulevard, he continued. "It's very different here at night, isn't it?" The variety of people along the beach during the day, everyone from tourists to fisherman, created a buzz of activity. At night, however, there were only occasional couples strolling along the bike lanes and the beach was nearly empty.

"I love the beach at night. It seems so peaceful and calm," Lauren replied.

"Have you ever spent the night on a boat?" Marc asked.

"No, although I imagine it would be fun."

"It just rocks you asleep," Marc answered.

Marc turned up the street that led to Lauren's apartment and pulled up outside of her home. "Here you go, all in one piece."

Lauren unfastened her seat belt and turned to say goodnight to Marc. She was surprised by his expression. Outside of the office he normally looked lighthearted and carefree, but tonight his expression was more serious. Tonight, when he looked at her it was obvious that he was very aware of her as a woman and Lauren caught her breath. Marc turned off the car engine, undid his own seat belt and took Lauren into his arms.

CHAPTER SIX

Lauren squinted as she awoke to the bright sun. The evening before had been late. Although she'd only had one glass of champagne with Leo to celebrate the successful closure of one of the firm's cases, she felt groggy. She could feel a headache threatening to come on full strength.

Slowly, she got up and started to get ready to run. She thought, hopefully, that getting out into the fresh air would make her feel better. After the episode the previous night she was almost glad that Marc was not joining her this morning. Almost.

Marc had kissed her with urgency and need, unlike any of the kisses she had exchanged with Jim. She had been surprised at first, but it hadn't taken her long to get over her initial shock and respond to his kiss.

The kiss had started out strong and firm before Marc had slowed, turning the kiss into a more probing and sensual exploration. She could feel her cheeks getting warm just thinking about it.

But then Marc had stopped and pulled away, quickly climbing out of the car and coming around to her side and opening the car door to help her out. Walking her to the front door of her apartment he asked for her key and unlocked the door.

Lauren was struggling to keep her wits about her and she scolded herself internally for being so responsive. She hadn't thought of Jim at all. She could only think of Marc's strong arms pulling her towards him. Lauren's cheeks felt warm and flushed and her knees were shaking.

Marc had unlocked the door and handed the keys back to her. He had a controlled look on his face and the twinkle that was usually crinkling little crow's feet around his eyes was replaced with a serious expression. "I refuse to apologize twice for kissing you tonight," he started. "It really wouldn't be a sincere apology since I can't say I regretted it either time," he finished, the twinkle in his eye flashing momentarily. And with that, he turned and walked away, leaving Lauren standing open-mouthed at her front door.

It took Lauren a little longer to get ready this morning as she rummaged around, looking for her running shoes. *How am I going to be able to look him in the eye at the office?* Lauren thought to herself as she stepped outside and turned to lock her front door. Things just hadn't been the same since he'd started at the firm. And last night! She'd done nothing to stop him.

Marc had left so abruptly. Of course, he would have had to return to the party to pick up Sylvia. He was probably regretting kissing her. It had probably been impulsive, nothing more.

One thing was certain as she started her morning stretching. She was going to end her dating relationship with Jim. Maybe she would be able to salvage a friendship with him, but after last night, it was obvious to Lauren that she would never be able to deepen her relationship with him. It wouldn't be fair to lead him on.

As she started to run, Lauren tried to put thoughts of Marc out of her mind. She had resolved to break up with Jim, but she was afraid to look any deeper at her feelings. She tried to convince herself that Marc had only helped her realize that a future with Jim was impossible. Certainly not that Marc meant anything to her or her to him. He couldn't, could he? After all, she'd only met him a month ago she rationalized to herself. Realizing that she was not successfully putting Marc out of her mind, she tried to concentrate on the activities around her.

Many of the artists were arriving to set up their artwork along Cabrillo Boulevard. The pieces that were already set up provided adequate distraction for Lauren.

There was always a variety of artwork. Watercolors, oils, photography, even sculpture and crafts. Lauren decided to take the time to explore after she circled the bird sanctuary.

As she started the loop around the private reserve she noticed several birds were skimming the surface of the pond and another flew overhead, squawking a solo song that sounded melancholy and lonely as the wind carried away the sound.

Lauren picked up the pace, trying to push the feeling of uneasiness away. Looking at the artwork would be a good distraction. It would probably be better to hurry back and take her time walking from one length of the art show to the other. Most of the artists showed their work every weekend, staking out a particular spot to display their work.

Usually Lauren ran in the morning before the artists were set up for the art show. As she wandered through the exhibits she realized that it had been some time since she'd last taken the time to look around. The crafts were set up along the eastern side of the beach and were the first stands that Lauren came upon after circling the bird sanctuary. There were children's toys made out of wood, embroidered pillows and macramé plant holders. But the stand that made Lauren stop and stare was the collection of wind chimes. There were a variety of sizes and shapes that chimed in the early morning breeze.

Lauren stood for several minutes letting the early morning breeze brush by her, cooling her down from her run. She saw one chime in particular that caught her eye. In many ways it was like all the others with a copper pipe hanging down in the center, but this one was different. It had additional, smaller copper pipes around the outside and several ceramic birds that appeared to be flying among the pipes. The sound was whimsical.

After spending a lot of money on the dress and shoes for the party the night before, purchases like the wind chime would have to wait. It was a pity, Lauren thought. She knew the perfect place to hang it...out in the small garden behind her apartment.

"Beautiful, isn't it?" asked a deep voice from beside her.

"Marc!" Lauren exclaimed as she turned to see him standing next to her. He was wearing a pair of jeans and a plaid flannel shirt open over a white t-shirt. The blue in the plaid shirt accented his eyes. Lauren wondered how he could transition so well between formal and casual clothes. It was hard for her to decide which she liked better. "I thought you were leaving for Los Angeles today?" she asked.

"I am. I just decided I'd leave a little later in the day. After spending time in Santa Barbara, it's hard to look forward to the crowds of a large city, especially when it comes to the freeways."

Lauren laughed. "Well, if you stay here long enough you'll soon be in a crowd of tourists that come up to see the artists' displays!"

Marc returned her laughter with a deep, rumbling laugh of his own. "I guess I can't win either way, then." He motioned for the artist to come over to where they were standing. "I guess I'll just have to make my purchase in a hurry so I can be on my way."

When the elderly craftsman came towards them Marc smiled and pointed to the wind chime that Lauren had been noticing earlier. In a matter of minutes the man had taken down the piece and wrapped it up in tissue paper. After he put it into a bag with plastic handles to make it easier to carry, he handed the bag to Marc who passed him several bills to cover the cost.

The tissue paper rustled in the plastic bag as Lauren and Marc started to walk down the boulevard looking at additional stands together. Lauren felt happy that Marc had liked the chimes, knowing that he would be able to enjoy their sound when she herself had not been able to afford them. She would be able get chimes for her garden another day.

They browsed through the displays without speaking. There was a variety of work and Lauren found most of it compelling. However, as they made it towards the end of one of the stands there were several dark canvases that made Lauren stop and stare. Marc stood quietly next to her for several minutes before asking "Not something that you'd like in your home is it?"

"I don't know...well actually, you're probably right. Not in my home but the work certainly is incredible. I can feel the anguish and pain of the woman painted. It makes me sad." Lauren felt like she was babbling as she looked closer at the canvas that depicted a woman alone in a dark room wearing a dark dress while she looked out a window at a dark, grey city beyond. In many ways the painting seemed out of place among all the colorful work they had seen previously. The palm trees and ocean in the background almost seemed an ironic backdrop to the painting.

"It must be awful to feel so alone," Lauren said as she felt a shiver pass through her body.

Marc put his arm around her shoulders, not knowing how to reply. It had occurred to him lately that she was right. It was an awful thing to feel alone. Before he'd met her it had never struck him as odd that he liked to travel around working on a variety of cases, but now he was beginning to realize how unfulfilling it was. It had been a long time since he'd felt the way he did when he was with Lauren.

"Come on, I've got a great idea. Why don't we go sailing like I promised you. The weather is great... just the right amount of wind to make it fun." Marc dropped his arm from Lauren's shoulders and pulled her by the hand towards the harbor. "Come on!"

Lauren laughed. It would be fun to sail away for the afternoon. "Alright, alright!" she replied. "But first, why don't I make us a lunch to take along. It's almost time to eat."

"That sounds great! Why don't we meet on the dock in half an hour? Does that give you enough time?"

"I think so. I'll see you soon." Lauren turned up the street that led to her apartment. She stopped and turned back towards Marc. "Wait a minute, what about Los Angeles?"

"Los Angeles can wait. This really is the perfect type of day to go sailing. I'll see you soon," Marc dismissed Lauren's concerns. She restarted the walk to her apartment.

"Hey, Lauren!" Marc called out to her and she turned again with a questioning look.

"What?"

"Actually, I bought this for you," Marc said as he held out the bag with the wind chime inside.

"For me?" She asked softly. Lauren felt shy as she walked back towards him.

"Yes, for you," Marc replied with a laugh. More seriously he said, "I wanted to say thank you for all the hard work you've been doing on the case. I really appreciate it."

Marc didn't add that he had wanted to give it to her after he'd seen her expression as she looked at the wind chimes. Before he'd approached her down by the beach, he'd caught her with an expression of wistful happiness mingled with awe and wonderment. He wanted to capture that expression and keep it with him always.

Lauren took the bag that Marc handed her, her hand brushing his softly in the transfer. "Thank you, it's beautiful." She didn't know what else to say as she turned again towards her apartment.

"I'll see you in half an hour!" Marc called after her, watching her walk away, a lightness lifting his heart to his throat.

The first thing Lauren did when she entered her apartment was to unwrap the wind chimes. She marveled again at the design as she walked out into the garden and removed a hanging plant from a hook on the overhead trellis and replaced it with the chimes. A light breeze brushed the pieces together and the musical sound drifted into the kitchen as Lauren hurried to put together a picnic basket.

It didn't take her long to prepare several sandwiches, pick out a variety of fresh fruit and make a pasta salad from some leftovers in her refrigerator. She added several cans of vegetable juice and a package of cookies and she had a picnic lunch all ready to go. She glanced at her watch. *Not bad,* she congratulated herself. She still had enough time to make sure Buster was fed and to change into clothes a little more suitable for sailing.

She changed quickly into a white tank top and covered it with a cotton denim blouse that she left unbuttoned and knotted at her waist. She also pulled on a pair of denim shorts that were cut long and slim. She grabbed a dark green sweater from the shelf in her closet and slung it over her shoulders, wondering if it was going to be cold enough to need it or not. Lauren looked at her feet. She was wearing a pair of white socks, but she didn't know what shoes to wear. She didn't own deck shoes and after looking through her closet she decided her running shoes were probably her best option.

Lauren looked at her watch again and realized she needed to hurry. She picked up the picnic basket she had packed, caught the sweater as it slipped off her shoulder and readjusted it around her neck.

As she pulled the door shut, locked up and put her keys into the flower box, she realized how excited she was about going sailing.

It didn't take her long to reach the dock and as she walked towards the craft her footsteps echoed on the wooden planks of the deck. The smell of salt water filled the air and Lauren felt exhilarated as she inhaled deeply.

Lauren saw Marc on board "My Only Love." He'd used the time apart to change as well. He was still wearing the plaid flannel shirt and t-shirt, but he'd changed into shorts and topsider deck shoes. He was busy untying the sails from the boom and they rustled in the light breeze as they were set free. Marc moved around the craft, checking various ropes and the rudder to make sure everything was in working order.

"Hi Lauren, come on aboard!" he greeted her with a wave that motioned her forward. He moved from the opposite side of the boat and came towards her to give her a hand. She jumped aboard onto the smooth, firm surface of the boat. Her feet were solidly on the deck, but the floating sensation as the boat rocked gently beneath her caught her off guard. *This was going to be unlike any experience I've had before,* she thought to herself.

"Have you ever been sailing before?"

"No, never."

"Well, then we'll have to go over a couple things before we start. Do you swim?"

"Yes, I used to be a camp lifeguard."

"Great. But you should know that all the cushions on the deck here are approved floatation devices." Marc motioned to several built-in bench structures on the boat that were covered with thick, blue cushions. "Also, there are life jackets in here," he said indicating a latched cabinet. "And below, as well. Let me give you the complete tour."

The next thirty minutes were spent looking around the boat and reviewing the information Lauren needed to know before they set sail. Marc showed Lauren how the sail operated and explained how the wind was used to move the craft. "Just remember, this boom that holds the main sail is going to swing back and forth, from one side of the boat to the other to propel us in the direction we want to go. That means, when I yell "Boom" be prepared to duck down low."

Lauren nodded, intent on listening to all of his instructions. There seemed to be so much to learn. "Don't worry, you'll do fine," Marc said reassuringly. "In no time at all we'll have made you into a sailor. Let's take the lunch down below and then we'll get started."

Marc picked up the picnic basket and led Lauren to a set of narrow steps that took them down into the hull of the craft. There was a small kitchen set up against the right, or as Lauren had learned, the starboard side. There was a small table on the left, or port side, of the craft opposite of the kitchenette. Also, at the front, or bow of the boat, was a small couch that Marc said could be converted into a bed for overnight trips.

Lauren noticed that Marc had to bend over when they were down in the hull of the craft because of his height. She felt that the ceiling was close overhead, but she had enough room to stand up straight. "Do you have trouble cooking down here?" Marc gave her a quizzical look. Lauren blushed as she continued, "I mean, because of your height?"

Marc laughed as he put the basket into the small refrigerator. "No, I'm pretty used to living on the boat. I spent a couple months living on her about a year ago. Although, I did try to spend as much time above on deck as I could." Marc turned toward Lauren. "Ready?"

"Sure," she replied and they started up the steps.

"Just remember, the boat is going to be pulled up on one side when the wind fills the sail. Don't worry, the boat won't capsize."

Marc jumped onto the deck and unwound the rope that tied the boat securely in the slip. He quickly coiled up the rope and jumped back onto the boat. After storing the rope properly, he headed over towards the engine that was used to maneuver them into the deeper water. The engine sputtered to life and Marc slowly guided the boat out of the slip. The water glistened with the reflection of the sun and the breeze felt cool and refreshing.

Lauren was excited as they made their way towards the open sea. Marc had been patient and thorough while explaining the process of sailing. She felt completely safe.

The boat rocked gently as they made their way out of the harbor. Once they made it out towards the open sea, Marc shut off the engine and checked the direction of the wind. He loosened the rope that kept the main sail anchored loosely around the boom and began to hoist the sail up the mast. The sail waved in the air and, after Marc adjusted the rudder, began to fill with air. "Here we go!" Marc yelled over the sound of the waves splashing against the side of the boat. The bow of the boat dipped into the waves and a spray of water splashed into the air.

Marc motioned for Lauren to join him on the port side of the boat. "Ok, now lean away from the sail. Here, watch." Marc anchored himself firmly, pulled on the main sail line, and leaned back as the starboard side of the boat skimmed the water.

Lauren could feel a dip in her stomach, just as if she were on an elevator plummeting downwards. She braced herself and leaned backwards, mimicking Marc's movement. It was exhilarating! She watched Marc adjust the rope, pulling it in and letting it out to maximize the wind to propel the boat, but soon the wind died down and the sail began to flutter in the wind.

"Hold on and duck down, we're going to tack around." Marc quickly maneuvered the boat to catch the wind on the other side of the sail. With a few flutters it filled with air and Marc pulled in the lead rope to tighten the sail.

Lauren had hovered as low as she could as the boom swung over her head and she joined Marc on the opposite side of the boat as the wind started to fill the sail.

Sailing! It was wonderful! Lauren looked across at the sail, billowing full with air and she laughed. "This is fun!" she said as she turned to Marc.

"I'm glad you like it." Marc smiled back at her. They both leaned backwards as the boat dipped lower and Lauren watched the water foaming as the boat cut through the surface.

Lauren's eyes traveled back towards Marc, noticing his dark, tan muscular legs next to her own slender ones.

They continued to tack along the coast of Santa Barbara, sailing a zig-zagging pattern along the coastline. After sailing a ways down the coast, Marc let the main line slacken and the wind slipped away from the sails.

"How about stopping for a bite to eat?" Marc asked. Lauren's cheeks were flushed with color and her eyes sparkled. "It's wonderful. I can't believe I've never tried this before!"

Marc pulled the sail down and tied it loosely around the boom. He also released the anchor to stabilize the boat. Even with the anchor lowered the boat bobbed on the surface of the water.

Marc led the way into the cabin and Lauren followed him as they made their way into the cabin below.

Marc opened a cupboard and pulled out several plates and glasses. Next he opened a drawer and extracted silverware, napkins and placements. Within minutes he had a table set for their picnic lunch.

Lauren noticed that everything was designed to fit securely in place. Pots and pans clipped onto the range, and elastic ties fastened dishes into the cabinets to avoid slippage. Lauren could not imagine what it would be like to cook in the kitchen anywhere but securely tied at the boat dock. The rocking of the boat was soothing and relaxing, but Lauren could only imagine the perils of cooking that would be created.

Lauren retrieved the picnic basket from the small refrigerator and helped Marc finish setting the table. She pulled out silverware from the drawer, making sure the elastic ties were still snapped securely around the remaining pieces of flatware.

"This looks amazing. I'd love to see what you could do with an hour." Marc said as he started to unpack the basket. "Sandwiches, salad, fruit..."

"Don't forget the juice and cookies." Lauren laughed. Inside she glowed with his compliment. Maybe one day she would be able to cook for him. *What am I thinking?* Lauren asked herself. *He's going to be gone in two months. Sooner if the case is settled.*

"What are you thinking?" Marc interrupted her train of thought.

"Nothing, really. I'm hungry, let's eat," Lauren answered and she picked up her sandwich and took a bite.

Marc looked skeptical as he picked up his sandwich, but he didn't pressure her to say more. Instead he switched topics. "I love sailing. The first time I went was when my father was stationed in Italy. I was fifteen years old and I didn't know which was more incredible, sailing or the Italian Riviera." Lauren enjoyed hearing about Marc's childhood. "But then my father was transferred to Arizona and I realized how much sailing meant to me. The two years we lived in the desert were the hardest for me. That's why I decided to go to college in Boston where I could do a lot of sailing."

Lauren noticed ruddiness in his cheeks and how good-looking it made him. *Sailing definitely suits him,* she thought.

They spent the majority of their lunch discussing the boat. Marc answered several questions that Lauren posed to him and the conversation stayed light and carefree.

After the meal, Marc picked up their dishes and washed them quickly in the little sink, ignoring Lauren's protests. "There's a cloth in that drawer...If you would like you can help me dry."

"Certainly, it's the least I can do." Lauren stood next to Marc and took the dishes one by one as Marc finished washing them and dried each one carefully. It was enjoyable to be here with Marc, watching his strong hands grip the plates and rinse them clean. Lauren found she couldn't stop herself from giggling. Her laughter was contagious and Marc laughed back, "What's so funny?"

"You. Look at the soap suds on your arm. Somehow, this wasn't what I pictured in my mind before we met, when I tried to picture the powerful attorney, Marcus Harland."

"Oh really...just what do you picture when you think of me now?" Marc asked softly.

Suddenly the little room seemed very close and intimate.

Lauren felt flustered as she finished drying the plate in her hand. "I don't know, just not a man hovering over a sink with his hands and arms covered with foamy suds."

"You know what I think of when I think of you, Lauren?"

When she didn't answer, he continued, "I think of a beautiful woman who deserves better than Jim Adamson." His kiss surprised her. His lips were soft as they brushed against hers. Lauren ached to lean closer to him, but she needed to explain. Needed to tell him that she'd already decided to break off her relationship with Jim, but suddenly he was pulling away.

"We need to start back. I have to get on my way to Los Angeles." Marc seemed distant and unapproachable and Lauren didn't know how to begin. Marc brushed past her and headed up to the deck. Lauren quickly finished drying the dishes and tried to secure everything before joining Marc on the deck.

When she made it upstairs, Marc was back to his usual self, but he was busy preparing the boat to sail. "Here, pull the sail up with this rope," Marc called over to her, as he tossed her the rope. Lauren was thankful to have something to do. She tried to watch Marc out of the corner of her eye and she saw him winding one of the ropes around a metal hook.

Within a few minutes they were sailing with the wind and Lauren could feel her hair lift from her neck and fly freely behind her. She tried to turn to face Marc, but her movement only caused her hair to fly across her face. She laughed as she struggled to remove the strands in front of her. A spray of water sent a spritz of mist across her face and Lauren was absorbed into the flow of the boat. All thoughts beyond sailing were temporarily gone from her mind.

All too soon the ride was over. They had tacked their way back towards the harbor, ducking the boom and shifting sides to accommodate the sail. Lauren had learned the differences of sailing with the wind and against the wind.

Marc had even allowed her to take control of the main line and showed her how to adjust the sail.

Marc had assured her that if she felt any fear she could always lessen the grip on the line and it would release the wind from the sail. Marc noticed that she never once opted to release the rope. When it came to sailing, Lauren seemed to have no fear. She reminded him of the first time he had gone out. Sailing always left him wanting more, never feeling completely satisfied unless he had captured the wind and brought the boat to the edge, when it seemed like a miracle that the boat didn't tip over.

After they eased the boat back into the harbor and secured it in the slip, Marc went below and retrieved the picnic basket.

"Thanks for the lunch. It was wonderful," he said as he handed her the basket.

"The ride was incredible. It wasn't like anything I've experienced before. Thank you," Lauren replied. She was beginning to feel awkward and she jumped onto the dock. "Have a good trip to Los Angeles."

"I'll try," Marc replied.

"How long are you going to be gone?"

"Several days. I should be back to the office on Thursday."

"Well, I'll see you then...and Marc, thanks again." Lauren turned and walked down the planks of the dock, the empty picnic basket swinging at her side.

CHAPTER SEVEN

When Lauren returned to her apartment after the sailing excursion there were two messages on her answering machine. One was from her mother and the other from Jim.

Lauren called her mother and chatted briefly about the sailboat ride. Helen Evans listened to her daughter's voice as she described the trip and she began to wonder how much of Lauren's excitement was due to the sailing and how much could be attributed to this man, Marc Harland.

Helen knew her daughter well and she would be patient. Lauren needed the time to work out her feelings, but Helen knew she would tell her all about him when the time was right.

Their conversation shifted to Lauren's job and attending law school. "Have you decided where you're going yet?" Helen asked her daughter. "I don't know much about the process, but aren't they expecting an answer from you soon?"

"Actually, Mom, I reserved a spot with both schools while I waited to hear about the financing. It was worth it to keep the positions open for me. If one of the schools isn't able to offer me enough money the decision will have been made for me and I may not have had a place at the school if I hadn't put down the deposit."

"Well, honey, I'm sure you'll be happy at either school." Helen was proud of her daughter's accomplishment. Getting into law school and receiving financial assistance was not easy. "When will you hear about the financing?" Lauren glanced over towards her coffee table. She'd received thick packets from both schools during the last several days and she had planned on examining them at length this weekend. Maybe she would have time after she got off the phone with her mother.

After assuring Lauren that everything was alright with her and her father, Helen rang off the line. When Helen replaced the receiver of the telephone, she realized that Lauren had not mentioned Jim during the entire call. "This is very interesting," Helen had chuckled to herself. "Marc Harland must be quite a man."

Lauren looked at the phone after hanging up with her mother. "I suppose I should call Jim back as well," she muttered to herself. She knew she would not change her mind about severing their relationship, but she didn't want to hurt his feelings. She picked the phone up and dialed Jim's number. It took several rings for Jim to answer and he sounded groggy and disoriented when he picked up the phone.

"Oh, hi Lauren. I've been trying to sleep off this hangover of mine." Jim groaned.

"Did you get home alright last night or did you stay at the Whitman's?" Lauren asked.

"I made it home," he replied but he didn't say how. Lauren was relieved to know that Leo wouldn't have let Jim drive.

"Look, Jim, I need to talk to you. Would you like to have dinner tonight?" After making arrangements to meet at a nearby restaurant, Lauren hung up the phone and reached for the large envelopes from the two different law schools.

The first envelope contained a cover letter and many colorful brochures. There was also a complete write up on the financial assistance that the California school would be able to offer. Lauren grinned. It was a very nice offer.

The second envelope was very similar, outlining the offer from the school in Michigan. Lauren, by completing her undergraduate education outside the state of Michigan, had forfeited her residency. It was clear that the California school had an advantage over the Michigan school because of her resident status.

Lauren continued to compare the two packages. All things considered, the two offers were very similar. *So much for the decision being made for me,* thought Lauren to herself.

Deep inside her heart she knew she preferred the school in Santa Barbara. However, she'd still not resolved her feelings of being closer to her parents as they got older.

Well, she still had a few weeks before she was required to make a larger deposit to secure her place.

Lauren sighed and looked at her watch. She'd better shower and get ready to meet Jim. Her confrontation with Jim was necessary but wasn't something she was looking forward to. She didn't want to hurt him, but she knew that delaying their discussion might only hurt him more later.

It was shortly after six when Lauren walked into the restaurant, cool and comfortable in a pair of jeans and cotton blouse. She saw Jim sitting at the bar almost immediately. As she approached she realized that he was drinking a cup of strong, black coffee.

"Oh...Hey, Lauren. How are you doing?" Jim looked a little awkward.

"I'm fine. Did you want to get a table?"

"Sure, but let's try to get one away from all these clattering dishes. I'm almost completely over this headache of mine, but I still seem sensitive to sounds."

After they were seated at a table tucked in the back of the restaurant, Lauren started. She felt a little uncomfortable. She realized too late, that having this conversation in a public place might not be the best idea, but it was better done now, at the onset of their meal, than waiting for the final course. She took a deep breath.

"Jim, I don't think we should see each other again, at least not to date..."

"Hey, look honey, is it because of last night? You know I don't drink usually, but...well...I felt so uncomfortable in that get up, I just needed to feel relaxed."

"No, Jim, that's not the reason, although it does seem you've been drinking rather heavily lately," she said softly.

"It's that attorney, isn't it? I bet you think he can offer you a better life, is that it?"

Lauren shook her head. "No, it's nothing like that. I just think that you and I are looking for something different. And it has struck me lately that I don't think I'll ever be able to offer you what you want."

"What is that supposed to mean?" Jim asked abruptly.

"It means I don't want a relationship with you," Lauren replied calmly. "I hope you understand. I think you are a wonderful person, but I think you'll be happier with someone who can give you the things you want." Lauren paused. "Someone who can give you what you want both mentally and physically."

Jim sighed. "I guess you're right. I just haven't wanted to admit it to myself. So is this the part when I say we can still be friends?"

Lauren laughed. "Actually, I thought that would be my line." Lauren felt relieved. She'd been concerned that the conversation might go badly, but Jim seemed calm and rational. It made Lauren think that he may have been thinking very similar thoughts already.

They finished their meal, talking about various topics. The remainder of their meal was between friends, nothing more. Maybe they would be able to maintain a friendship; however, Lauren was realistic. They would be able to be friends as long as no other woman entered Jim's life. Until then she would be able to enjoy his company.

Lauren had walked to the restaurant, but since it was getting late, Jim offered to drive her the short distance to her apartment. Lauren was surprised when he pulled up and stopped the engine.

"Actually, Lauren, there's something I guess I should tell you. I wasn't going to at first, but now..."

"What is it, Jim?"

"I just thought you should know that I've met someone. Nothing serious, but now, considering tonight, I think

I'm going to pursue something with her. I feel better telling you about it."

Lauren sat quietly for a moment. It was certainly not what she'd expected to hear and the news stunned her. She was surprised by her reaction, or more realistically, her lack of reaction. She didn't feel jealous in the least. She'd thought that she might feel a twinge of regret when Jim started dating another woman, but she felt nothing. Nothing at all. Her lack of emotion regarding his statement startled her. She turned towards Jim.

"You're upset aren't you?" he asked. "I shouldn't have told you."

Lauren placed her hand on his arm. "No, Jim. I'm glad you did. And I wish you all the best." She opened the car door and slid out of her seat. "Thanks for the ride home. Goodnight, Jim."

It was still relatively early when Lauren unlocked her door and went inside her apartment. One of the burdens hanging over her head was resolved and she felt a lightness in her step that she hadn't had for days. Now all she had to do was decide which law school she was going to attend and everything would be taken care of.

Lauren picked up the law book that was on her coffee table and started to read, preparing for the week ahead. She found it was difficult to concentrate. *I wonder why Marc went to Los Angeles?* It occurred to Lauren that he was probably lining up his next case, getting ready to move on away from Santa Barbara. The thought made her feel sad.

The next few days passed slowly for Lauren. Leo had called her into his office on Monday morning and confirmed that Marc was in Los Angeles pursuing another environmental case that was scheduled to start shortly after the completion of the Consumer Energy case. With his prolific knowledge and extensive experience, Marc had a lot to offer any firm with an environmental case coming to trial.

"I haven't given up yet, Lauren," Leo had said. "Just because he's being wined and dined by another firm doesn't mean we can't sweeten the pot."

Lauren was skeptical. You didn't make a man like Marc Harland change his mind easily. *Also, he was so clear the first day they had gone to lunch,* Lauren thought. His plan was to pursue several more individual cases and then open his own practice. Lauren was sure Marc wouldn't be interested in joining a firm as an associate. Lauren could think of nothing that would have changed during the last few weeks that would cause Marc to feel any differently.

"Lauren, are you feeling alright?" Leo broke through her reverie.

"What? Oh...sure Leo, I feel fine," Lauren answered absentmindedly. She tried to ignore the sudden knots that had taken over her stomach.

Lauren's run each morning seemed long and painful. She used to savor her time alone, but now she struggled to get out of bed and struggled to push herself to run the length of the beach and back.

She hadn't realized how quickly Marc had become a part of her morning routine. They always laughed together and on several occasions Marc had surprised her with bagels or doughnuts after their run. Without him beside her the five miles seemed to drag on forever.

Wednesday morning Lauren climbed into the shower after her run and let the cool water wash over her, willing it to wake and revitalize her. Lauren felt sluggish and slow this morning. *This must be depression setting in because of the breakup with Jim. I knew it was something I needed to do, but I'm probably experiencing a mourning period,* she thought to herself.

Lauren got dressed slowly and leaned down to scratch Buster behind the ears. "You're great, Buster. You are always there for me." Buster purred his response. After making sure he had food and water outside on the back porch, she let him out for the day. She called out her standard goodbye and closed the door. Buster was already making his way out of the yard. *It must be nice to be so carefree,* Lauren thought.

Lauren picked up her things and started to walk to the office. She had been doing the final research on the case and it was scheduled to go to court the following week. The case was expected to last several weeks and then there would be the final filings and settlement to resolve once a verdict had been made. Overall, it would be approximately six more weeks and then Marc would be leaving Santa Barbara. Lauren dragged her feet as she headed toward the office.

Usually the walk to her office took Lauren ten minutes, but this morning it was almost twenty minutes later before Lauren entered the tiled entranceway and walked past the koi pond.

She pressed the elevator button and watched the old dial above the doors monitor the movement between floors. Several minutes later, the bell chimed and the doors slid open and Lauren stepped aboard. It already felt like it was going to be a long, hard day.

Lauren checked with Julie for messages, put her things in her office and headed for the library. As she pushed open the heavy glass doors, she was startled as she almost crashed into the person exiting. A white, crisp shirt and suspenders filled her vision and as she looked up to apologize she looked into familiar deep blue eyes that had greeted her weeks before.

"Marc!" she exclaimed. "You're back! I didn't think you were going to return until tomorrow." She suddenly felt lighthearted. It seemed that all the emotion she had been holding in the last few days was about to bubble over.

"Hey, Lauren," Marc replied softly and Lauren took a step back. Suddenly the smell of his aftershave, the crispness of his shirt and the whole maleness permeating the air around him overwhelmed her and she needed to steady herself as she realized that her legs were shaking.

"My negotiations ended a little earlier than I anticipated, so I returned a day early," Marc continued. Lauren looked up, her eyes meeting his and she noticed a softness in his eyes. Normally his eyes sparkled with exuberance as he went about embracing life, but today there was something more, something gentle. "Did you miss me?"

Lauren got flustered. The closeness of his body and the seeming intimacy that surrounded his casual question caused her to stutter.

"Well...uh...su...urre," she started. "Th..The case is coming up on a criti...cal stage."

Marc sighed as he pulled away. It was obvious to him that Lauren only saw him as an attorney that she worked with on a case, nothing more. Jealousy flared inside him as he thought of Jim. *The other man doesn't even know what he has,* Marc thought to himself. He tried to put a rein on his emotions and focus on the work in front of him. The trial date was only a week away.

They worked together, side by side for the majority of the morning. Lauren was surprised by her renewed energy, but she noticed that Marc seemed distant, almost distracted. Regardless, his research was perfect. He even took the time to explain the strategy of the upcoming case to her. Even though they had outlined the basic premise of the case, Lauren appreciated that he always took the time to fill her in on the finer details.

It was late morning when Leo pushed open the doors and entered the law library.

"Good, good, both of you are here. We just found out that Judge Rollins will be residing over the proceedings. He's a tough cookie, but he's fair and he seems to understand the finer elements of the law."

"That's great, Leo," Lauren replied. Looking at the faces of the two men she added, "Isn't it?"

"Sure." Leo responded, patting Marc on the back. "It just means that Marc has his work cut out for him."

"Well, Leo, I think the case will speak for itself," Marc replied calmly. "Are you free for lunch, Leo? There are a couple of things I'd like to discuss with you."

"I think so, but let me check my calendar just to be sure. Shall we head to my office?" Leo replied and before receiving an answer he started towards the door.

"I'm right behind you, Leo." Marc turned towards Lauren. "We'll finish this after lunch. You don't mind do you?"

"No, not at all. Have a good lunch." Lauren watched the two men as they left the library. "He's probably working out his departure schedule with Leo," Lauren muttered to herself. She could feel her depression coming back. She decided she should get out of the law library and out of the office into the fresh air outside.

It only took her several minutes to retrieve her purse and catch the elevator. Once she was on the street she walked briskly to the courthouse. She headed up Anacapa Street towards the main archway that led to the sunken gardens.

Lauren wandered awhile, reading the plaques like she'd done so many times before, but today the names weren't sinking in and her mind was miles away. It took several minutes before she realized that someone was calling her name.

"Lauren!...LAUREN!"

She turned quickly, flustered, wondering how long her name had been called, suddenly aware of how lost in thought she'd become. "Jim!" she exclaimed in surprise. Although his office was nearby she couldn't remember when she'd seen him at the courthouse last.

"Hey, kid. I've been calling your name. You must have been miles away."

Lauren felt her cheeks warm. "Sorry about that. Say, what are you doing here?"

"Actually, I was going to grab a sandwich at the deli across the street and then I saw you," Jim replied. "Thought I'd come over and say hi."

They began to make the rounds of the garden perimeter and they talked casually. Lauren was surprised at how easily they slipped into a comfortable friendship. She enjoyed Jim now that the pressures of a relationship had been removed.

"Do you want to join me for a sandwich?"

Lauren looked at her watch. It was later than she thought. "I really need to get back to the office, but I'll walk over with you. I think I'll get a sandwich to take back with me."

"Great, let's go," Jim replied. He was so carefree, his spirits high. Lauren felt a tug of depression pull at her. She tried to shake her uneasiness and she laughed at a joke Jim shared with her. The laugh caught in her throat as they approached the restaurant. Lauren saw Marc and Leo exiting. Her eyes caught Marc's gaze and she couldn't break away.

Marc's eyes seemed to get cold as he looked at her and then towards Jim who was still laughing over his anecdote.

Lauren stumbled outside the restaurant and Jim reached out to catch her from falling. Lauren was thankful for his assistance but felt that his closeness conveyed a false sense of intimacy.

"Hello, Jim. Lauren," Marc said as he brushed past. Leo stopped and chatted for a minute while Marc waited impatiently beside him.

"Lauren, if you could bring those notes by this afternoon, I'd appreciate it. Jim, it's good to see you again." As he turned to join Marc he added, "Enjoy your lunch."

The encounter with Leo and Marc made Lauren uncomfortable and she fidgeted as she ordered her sandwich.

"Are you sure you don't want to eat here?" Jim asked.

Lauren looked at her watch again and decided to stay. "Alright, but it'll have to be quick."

Lauren had a hard time relaxing during lunch. She didn't know why she was so bothered by running into the two men on the way into the restaurant. Fortunately, Jim didn't seem to notice and the lunch passed with him filling in most of the conversation.

As Lauren pushed open the heavy door leading into the law firm, she saw Marc and she could feel her heart in her throat. The sight of him made her pulse quicken and she felt flushed.

The clumsiness she sometimes felt around Marc seemed to overtake her again and it occurred to her that it was very important to her what Marc thought of her. She realized that it bothered her to think that Marc could have possibly misunderstood the earlier interaction with Jim. Inwardly she groaned. *Why would he think anything else? I'm supposed to be dating Jim.*

Lauren hurried towards her office and shut the door. She took several deep breaths and tried to steady her nerves. *I'm in love with him,* she scolded herself. *How could I have been so foolish?*

Suddenly her depression seemed to make sense. She wasn't depressed about breaking up with Jim. She'd been depressed that Marc hadn't been around. She realized how much Marc had infiltrated her life and now she wanted him to be a part of it every day.

Lauren spent several minutes in her office, straightening the papers and files on her desk and trying to take her mind off of Marc. She was going to have to venture outside of her office sooner or later that afternoon to see Leo, but she was afraid she would run into Marc.

Lauren was feeling a little fragile now that she'd acknowledged the source of her anguish over the past several days. Falling in love with Marc Harland had knocked her off of her feet. "When did this happen?" she pondered to herself, as she rearranged the pencils in the cup on top of her desk for the second time.

Realistically she knew she'd fallen into those deep blue eyes the first day they had met. But falling deeper into love had come about gradually and slowly as she got to learn more about Marc. So gradually in fact that she felt she had just been hit over the head with the sudden reality.

It was almost as if she'd been looking for something and it wasn't where she thought it would be, but when she looked again she realized that it had been there all along.

Lauren turned towards her computer and pulled up the file Leo had wanted to see and sent the document to the printer. When the pages had stopped flowing into the paper tray, she picked them up and headed for Leo's office.

Leo's secretary was nowhere to be seen and Leo's door was open. Lauren approached cautiously and knocked on the door. Leo pivoted around in his chair and beckoned her into his office.

"Lauren, my dear. How are you?" he asked. After they exchanged normal salutations, he continued. "Ah! I see you brought me the notes on the Consumer Energy case."

For the next several minutes, the two of them combed through the file. "Good, good, Lauren. Marc and I discussed strategy over lunch today and I think we've got a good chance at winning this case."

"I agree. The research seems to back up our point of view." Both Lauren and Leo knew that the law could be interpreted in various ways. Logically, though, the Consumer Energy case seemed to be falling into place. Future offshore drilling would be halted if they won. It was exciting to Lauren to think of the ramifications.

"Lauren, how are you getting along with Marc these days?"

"Well, he's been out of town for the last several days, but everything seems fine. Anything wrong?" Lauren asked, concerned.

"No, not at all." Leo quickly assured her. "As I mentioned before, I want to sweeten the pot to encourage Marc to stay with the firm."

Lauren let out the breath she was holding since Leo had mentioned Marc's name and tried to relax.

"The firm has a membership at the Santa Barbara Polo Club. The season is about to start and I thought we could take Marc to one of the matches. The action on the polo field is incredible!"

Lauren knew about the firm membership at the club, but she'd never actually attended an event. The club membership was maintained for the partners of the firm. When an associate was included it was considered an honor and almost a coup on the part of the associate.

"I'm sure Marc would enjoy that very much," Lauren replied.

"Good, good. Then it's settled. We'll take Marc to a match if he wants to go."

"We?"

"Sure, you, me and Lily," Leo replied. "The two of you seem to work well as a team. It makes sense that you would come with us."

Lauren felt excited about the excursion. Marc might not realize the significance of the invitation, but Lauren did. Anyone who had worked for the firm for any length of time knew the significance of being invited to attend as a member of the firm. The matches were open to the public so anyone could attend, but the firm invitation was special.

"When is the match, Leo?" Lauren asked.

"Not this coming Sunday, but the following one. There are games every Sunday through October, but with the trial starting a week from Monday, I'd like to get Marc to the Polo Club before he's absorbed with the case," Leo replied. "Also, I want to make sure he doesn't accept any other offers," he added with a grin.

"I look forward to it," Lauren said as she stood up to leave the office.

Leo stopped her before she could leave. "Actually, Lauren, I didn't mean to exclude Jim. He's more than welcome to attend as well."

"Jim and I aren't seeing each other anymore but thank you for asking."

"What! What happened? How are you doing? Can I help with anything?" Leo stood up and came around his desk while asking his string of questions, not giving Lauren enough time to respond to any of them.

"We're still friends, Leo, but we decided that we were looking for different things. And I'm doing fine. Just do me a favor and don't mention it to anyone right now."

Leo looked puzzled. "Of course not, if that's what you want."

"I just don't want to answer a lot of questions, Leo," Lauren said. "I'm doing fine, really. I just don't want anyone feeling sorry for me."

Leo nodded his reply. He'd noticed she'd been moping around the office for the last several days. It hadn't occurred to him that she might have broken it off with Adamson. Leo was relieved. He'd never understood their relationship anyway.

As Lauren turned again towards the door to Leo's office she found herself face to face with Marc. She felt like she was bumping into him every time she turned around today.

"Good, good, Marc, I'm glad you're here. I was just telling Lauren about the Polo season at the Santa Barbara Polo Club. How would you like to join us for a match a week from Sunday?" Leo asked.

As Leo and Marc exchanged details about the upcoming match, Lauren tried to steady her shaking legs. *How am I going to get through this?* she groaned to herself. *With poise and self-respect,* she answered herself as she raised her chin slightly with a determined air.

Lauren tried to concentrate on the conversation the two men in front of her were having. Marc's close proximity and the spicy scent of his aftershave made it difficult for Lauren to think of anything but removing Marc's clothing piece by piece, but she had to remember where she was and remember who she was. The problem was that Marc made her think of things she'd never thought of before. Certainly she'd never felt any type of temptation throughout her relationship with Jim.

Lauren sighed to herself. Here she was, in love with a man who was going to walk out of her life in six weeks' time. A man who thought she was already involved with someone else and had no interest in her. The thought made her heart ache.

And here she stood, wondering what it would be like to loosen Marc's tie, slip apart the knot and pull the tie free.

How could she let Marc know that she and Jim were no longer dating? It wasn't really something that she could say casually, without a reason. "Oh, yes, and by the way Marc, just so you know, Jim and I aren't dating anymore," seemed awkward. Also, it was apparent to Lauren that Marc was dating Sylvia anyway and certainly he wasn't looking to settle down right now either.

Lauren wondered what it would be like, after removing Marc's tie, to pull his shirt open. She could almost hear the buttons popping away from their buttonhole enclosures to reveal his strong, muscular chest. If she could only reach out and touch Marc's smooth skin...

The two men were now discussing the Consumer Energy case and Marc turned toward Lauren. "Don't you agree, Lauren?" With a start, Lauren realized she had no idea what the question referenced or how to answer. She could feel her palms get sweaty as she searched for a suitable reply.

"I'm sorry, what was that?" she finally asked after unsuccessfully grasping for the wisps of the conversation that had been floating around her.

Marc was quick to respond. "Don't you agree that we've pretty much finished with the research and are ready to finalize our approach?

"Oh, yes, very much so," Lauren answered quickly. She hastily picked the pieces of Marc's clothing up off the floor of her mind and excused herself from the conversation.

CHAPTER EIGHT

So much for being poised and professional, Lauren thought to herself as she raced down the hall, away from Leo's office. Luckily the week was almost over and she could get away from everything for a while.

It wasn't like Lauren to feel the need to run away from her problems, but she was feeling overwhelmed. Between Marc and Jim, the upcoming case and deciding where to go to law school, Lauren felt exhausted.

On the spur of the moment she dug her personal black leather telephone book out of her purse and picked up the receiver of her office telephone. It only took her a minute to flip through the book to find the number she wanted. After dialing it, she waited for the line to connect. It was only several rings before the call was answered.

"Mariana?"

"Lauren! It's been ages. How have you been?" answered Lauren's friend. The two had met while they were taking an introductory political studies class their first year and had stayed in touch ever since. They'd even shared an apartment for the last two years of college, but when Mariana had been offered a job in Los Angeles she'd moved and Lauren had found the one bedroom apartment she was currently living in.

After several minutes of small talk, Lauren took a deep breath. "Mariana, do you have plans this weekend? I would love to get away for a day or two. Are you free?"

"Sure, I'd love to get together for the weekend. Do you want to come down here or do you want me to come up there?"

Lauren was thankful that her friend was free. She felt fortunate to have a friend like Mariana that she could call on a moment's notice. Their friendship withstood the ups and downs of their lives and even when there were gaps in their contact it always seemed like they had talked only hours earlier rather than not having talked in the days, weeks or months that had actually elapsed.

"I'd rather come down, if that's alright," Lauren replied.

"That sounds great. Tell me...is this an "I need to get away and rest" weekend or is it an "I want to be so busy that I can't think" weekend?"

Lauren laughed. "To be honest, I'm not sure. I just know I need to get away."

"No problem, we'll play it by ear," Mariana responded and after confirming the time and place to meet, they both hung up.

Lauren felt a sense of relief knowing she would be distracted for the weekend. She tried to ignore the little inner voice inside her that scolded her for running.

Now that she'd made her decision to flee to Los Angeles for the weekend, Lauren was able to focus on the work in front of her. The rest of the afternoon passed quickly and shortly after five Lauren put her telephone book back into her purse, gathered up her things and headed for the door.

As she headed for the elevator she almost bumped into Marc for what seemed like the umpteenth time that day. "I'm sorry. I don't think I've been watching where I'm going all day," Lauren apologized.

"No problem. You're heading out?"

"Yup. Did you need me to do anything for you before I go?" Lauren asked.

"No. Unless you would like to join me for dinner this evening?" Marc replied casually.

Before Lauren had a chance to reply, Julie came around the corner of the hallway and called to Marc. "Oh great, Marc, I found you. Sylvia is on the phone. She insisted that I find you. Can you take the call?"

Marc hesitated slightly. "Can you wait a minute? I'll be right back."

Lauren nodded and she watched Marc follow Julie down the hall.

"You can take the call at my desk if you'd like Marc," Lauren heard Julie say as they rounded the corner.

Lauren shifted her weight from one foot to the other while she waited for Marc to return. She could hear the deep tones of his voice echo around the corner, not audible enough to make out the conversation.

Within a few minutes Marc walked around the corner and rejoined Lauren. He didn't have his usual lighthearted look on his face and instead he looked all business.

"I'm sorry, Lauren. I have to renege on my dinner offer. Maybe another time?"

Lauren felt jealousy towards Sylvia overwhelm her. Marc obviously was going to meet the blond instead. Lauren tried to sound casual as she responded. "Well, since I never officially accepted, you're not officially canceling."

"Hey, well we can go out another time. Maybe tomorrow. I'm sorry, but I need to meet Sylvia now," Marc replied, confirming Lauren's worst fears and she could feel the jealousy surfacing again, causing her to bristle.

"Don't worry about it...really." She said as calmly as she could. She hoped Marc didn't notice anything unusual about her.

"Well, I'll meet you in the morning for our run, alright?"

"Sure, see you then." Lauren pushed open the heavy office doors that led to the elevator and prayed that the doors would open soon to whisk her away. Away from the heartache and pain she felt inside.

Lauren was thankful for the walk ahead of her. She walked with brisk determination, focusing only on reaching her destination. She pushed all thoughts of Marc and Sylvia out of her mind.

Buster was on the doorstep and he greeted her with a friendly "Meow."

"You're my buddy, Buster. What would I do without you?" Lauren said to him as she let her cat inside the apartment.

Lauren was late meeting Marc the following morning. She'd tossed and turned all night long and finally had fallen asleep around four in the morning. She'd dreamt that Marc had been coming towards her, but suddenly Sylvia appeared in her dream with her arm linked through Marc's, dressed in her crisp linen suit, every hair in place. Lauren woke with a start, trying to shake the dream from her mind. The buzz of her alarm clock helped bring her into reality and when Lauren leaned over to turn it off, she realized that it had been ringing for quite some time.

So now she was late. As she hurried toward the harbor she hoped that she looked alright. She didn't have the time to conceal the circles under her eyes, darkened by the lack of sleep. She was thankful that they ran side by side so Marc wouldn't see the dark shadows.

"Good morning, Lauren! I was beginning to wonder if you were going to make it," Marc greeted her cheerfully.

Lauren mumbled apologies while trying not to look at him and started to stretch. "I'll be ready in a few minutes."

The air was cool and Lauren took deep breaths as she stretched, feeling the air fill her lungs and send energy to her tired limbs. It didn't take her long to complete her warm-up exercises and a few minutes later they were on their way.

Lauren was thankful when she saw the bird sanctuary coming up on the left. The lack of sleep the night before was taking its toll on her this morning. Marc, however, was full of energy this morning. It bothered Lauren to think that Sylvia could be the cause of this heightened energy level in Marc. She knew that if she saw any future for her and Marc she too would probably feel an energetic high.

"Come on, Lauren, let's run this way." Marc prodded her gently towards the road that led towards the Biltmore.

"I don't know Marc. I'm tired. I didn't sleep very well last night..."

Marc continued to push her towards the lane. "Come on! I promise we'll take a break before we start back. It'll be fun."

Lauren pushed her tired body forward and laughed, partially at herself. "Slave driver!"

"So I guess you don't want to race me to the end of the block, do you?" Marc laughed back.

"NO!" Lauren tried to push her tired legs forward. As she ran she could feel the tingling in her muscles as they were pushed towards the limit of their endurance.

"Let's turn up here," Marc said as he sprinted ahead of her. Lauren groaned inwardly, praying that they would stop or turn back soon.

Marc must have read her mind because he called over his shoulder, encouraging her forward. "We'll stop at the end of the street, I promise!"

Lauren pushed forward, concentrating solely on reaching the end of the street. She didn't notice the narrow tree-lined street as she took each step towards the end of the block. She only noticed the dark pavement that seemed to stretch on and on.

Just when Lauren thought the street would never end, she looked up and saw the street end with a circular flourish. She started to laugh. Marc had led her towards the end of a cul-de-sac. There was nowhere else to run without turning around. Lauren took deep breaths as she slowed and bent forward, bracing her arms against her legs, exhausted. She started walking in a large circle, following the circumference of the pavement, to avoid muscle spasms.

"I told you we'd take a break," Marc said as they walked to cool down. "What do you think?" he asked as he gestured to the lot in front of them.

Lauren looked around her for the first time. The length of the little lane they had run was lush and green, with little bungalow style houses nestled off to the sides of the street. However, at the end of the street to one side of the cul-de-sac was a driveway that was flanked by several trees that led to a Cape Cod style cottage overlooking the water. The house was small and cozy with a beautiful rose garden to one side. There were lush, green plants and flowers all around the house. It was a perfect setting.

"Well?" Marc asked.

"It's...it's incredible," Lauren replied after searching for suitable words to describe the house. The view left her speechless. The house was everything she'd ever dreamed of and Lauren felt a feeling of wistfulness take over her. Someday she would be able to afford a home like this one, but she had to get through law school first.

Lauren turned to Marc. "Did you know this was here?"

"Yes, actually, I saw it for the first time yesterday and I wanted to see your reaction."

"You wanted to see my reaction?" Lauren repeated. "Why?" Lauren was surprised to see Marc get flustered.

"I just wanted to see if you had the same reaction to this place as I did," he answered. Before Lauren had a chance to question him further, he continued. "It's getting late. Do you feel rested enough to start the run back?"

"Sure." Lauren was feeling re-energized. The house in front of her made her feel an unexplainable feeling of joy and happiness. The turbulent feelings she'd been having the past several days seemed to temporarily lift away. "I'll race you to the corner."

"You're on!" Marc replied as Lauren started to run. "Hey, what ever happened to ready, set, go?" he laughed as he followed her.

"I figured I needed every advantage I could get." Lauren laughed over her shoulder and she let out a little yelp as she realized how close Marc was to her. She pushed forward harder and they ended up crossing the imaginary finish line at the same time.

Marc was laughing and calling for a rematch. Lauren laughed back, feeling carefree. If only she could bottle the day and have it with her forever. She loved Marc, loved him as he was with her today, running with her side by side. She loved working with him, loved being with him. Together they were a good team, fighting for a good cause. Lauren felt the happiness slip away as she thought of Marc with Sylvia. Lauren would have to say goodbye to Marc soon, she thought bitterly.

"I didn't tell you, I'll be out of town this weekend," Lauren said. "So I won't be able to meet you to run until Monday."

"Oh, anything special planned?" Marc asked casually.

"I'm visiting a friend of mine in Los Angeles," Lauren replied, trying to keep her voice light.

"Kind of ironic. Me just getting back and now you going. Los Angeles doesn't seem like the city for either one of us."

"Yeah, it is kind of ironic," Lauren agreed. "But I really like the city. It can be a lot of fun. There's always a lot to do..."

"Well, you'll have to show me the city you know because while I was there, I didn't have any fun at all," Marc said as they finished the last stretch of the return run to the harbor. "I'll see you later," he continued and turned to go.

Lauren hurried to her apartment and showered and changed to get into the office. It was a lot later than she thought and she decided to drive. She'd packed a bag the night before to prepare for her trip to visit Mariana and she picked it up, along with her briefcase, as she walked towards her front door. It probably made more sense to head straight to Los Angeles after she left the office later that day.

With that in mind, Lauren put both bags down and headed towards the back door of her apartment. She checked to make sure that Buster had enough food to last him through the weekend and then returned to the front door, gathered up the items she'd dropped and locked the door as she left her home.

The long day stretched before her and she was looking forward to her weekend getaway. She'd packed all the materials from both law schools and hoped to get some feedback from her friend.

Soon it was time to file the notes on the new case she was assigned. It was preliminary data gathering on a case that would soon fill her days after the completion of the Consumer Energy trial. With the majority of the research completed on the Consumer Energy trial, her days were spent working on both cases. When the trial started, Marc would need her on call for additional research to combat any unexpected twists throughout the trial so she was pushing to complete as much work on the new case as she could.

She was glad for the distraction, but while flipping through the thick bound volumes in the library completing her task, there were times when she needed to reference a case cited for the Consumer Energy trial. The research was a constant reminder of the time that she and Marc had spent together side by side in the library.

Lauren gathered up her purse and briefcase and headed for the elevator. It was only four-thirty, but she wanted to beat some of the commuter traffic that was usually heavier on Fridays. Everything around her reminded her of Marc. She was thankful that she would be able to escape to a city where they had no memories together, a place she could truly escape his presence.

The drive took a little over two hours, with the traffic moving fairly smoothly until she hit the outskirts of the San Fernando Valley. The traffic always seemed to bottleneck in Woodland Hills.

The traffic on 405 South was bumper to bumper and Lauren was thankful she wouldn't be on the freeway for long. Her friend had an apartment in Westwood Village, south of the University of California Los Angeles campus. The village was full of movie theaters, restaurants, students and young professionals. Lauren could see why her friend was attracted to this neighborhood.

There were many tall office buildings along Wilshire Boulevard and Lauren found herself wondering if the law office Marc had met with was located in any of these buildings. They were all relatively new and had impressive marble entrances, large chandeliers and well-dressed parking attendants, all signaling a level of success. Santa Barbara seemed to be very suburban by comparison and Lauren wondered if Marc would prefer a city like Los Angeles.

The sun was beginning to set as she drove along the wide boulevard and she could see the sparkling lights of the large theater marquee beckoning to her. There were large, bigger than life-sized pictures of a variety of well-known actors advertising their latest releases. Tom Hanks, Sandra Bullock and Keanu Reeves were several of the actors depicted in front of her. Lauren found herself wondering if she would be able to see any of the stars here in the movie capital of the world.

Mariana had told her that many people thought that all of the movie business took place in Hollywood, but she'd found studio business deals occurred throughout the city. A variety of posh restaurants like Morton's in West Hollywood, lush hotel suites in Beverly Hills or on studio lots in Burbank, Century City or West Los Angeles, the business aspects of the film industry were all around. Hollywood itself, especially along Hollywood Boulevard, were all more of a tourist attraction than a business destination.

Lauren drove down the quiet street that led towards Mariana's apartment. The younger professionals that lived in Westwood tended to live southeast of the campus because many of the fraternity and sorority houses were located on the northeast side of Westwood Village. It only took a few minutes to find a parking place and collect her things and soon Lauren was ringing her friend's apartment from the security phone.

Her friend answered quickly and buzzed Lauren into the building. "Come on back. It's the apartment to the left of the pool."

Lauren made her way through the courtyard that was lush and tropical with a variety of blooming plants. There were several tables and chairs set among the garden setting and water cascaded down a fountain facade.

Mariana opened the door to her apartment and came out to meet Lauren. She took the overnight bag from Lauren and pulled her by the hand into her apartment.

"I'm so glad you came down this weekend," started the long string of exclamations from her friend which ended with both of them falling onto the couch, laughing.

"Let me see if I got all that... I'm glad I came down too, dinner sounds good, I'd love to meet the man you've been dating, the play tomorrow sounds like fun, and no I don't have anything to wear to the after-party tomorrow night." Lauren laughed in response to the flood of questions Mariana had asked.

Mariana was shorter than Lauren, although a respectable height of five seven. She had short blond hair, hazel eyes and a beautiful smile. Her bubbly personality always attracted men to her and Lauren had a tough time keeping track of the latest beau in Mariana's life.

Mariana was a production coordinator and worked primarily on commercials. Her high energy and good spirits contributed to her success and she was always in demand. She and Lauren laughed at the irony of her career and undergraduate degree.

"At least law has some connection to Political Science. But, production coordinator?" Mariana would laugh. "No one expects me to be able to spout off the history of Marxism or the components of democracy, but it's fun to keep people on their toes!"

"Well, the futon couch you are sitting on folds out into a lovely queen size bed and is the closest thing I've got to a guest room," Mariana said, starting off the tour of her apartment. "I think I've added the bookcases since you were here last, and I also created a drawing space where the breakfast area used to be. It was the only place I could fit my drafting table." Mariana laughed.

Lauren followed her friend around the small one bedroom apartment, noticing the new curtains and throw pillows that had been added since the last time she'd been down. "The place looks great."

"Thanks, hon, but don't get too comfortable, we have to meet Daniel and his friend at eight o'clock."

"What friend?"

"Oh, didn't I tell you? Daniel has a friend he's bringing along to round out the party. Don't worry, it's not a date," Mariana replied. "Unless you want it to be one."

Lauren groaned. Well, she'd come to Los Angeles for distraction and it looked like her friend was trying to help. "I'm not interested in dating anyone right now."

"Fine, no problem then, it's not a date," her friend replied amicably. "But I hope before the weekend is over that you tell me what is going on," and before Lauren could answer, her friend added, "And, before you tell me nothing is going on remember I've known you a long time and I know better."

Lauren tried to laugh. "Alright, alright. I promise I'll tell you, but right now I'm starving."

"Dinner awaits, my dear, we just have to get to the restaurant." Mariana was secretly glad that her friend had an appetite. Things couldn't be all that bad.

"Let me change and we'll go," Lauren replied and within a few minutes they were heading for the door.

The dinner with the two men turned out to be very pleasant. Daniel and his friend, Patrick, were fun and interesting dinner companions.

Both men were architects and worked together at an architectural firm located in Santa Monica, one of the beach communities southwest of Westwood. Lauren found the stories they told about the process of designing houses for a variety of clients surprisingly entertaining. The two men obviously knew each other well and their conversation was light and carefree.

Lauren was happy for her friend. It was obvious that Mariana was very much in love with the sandy haired man sitting next to her and it appeared that Daniel felt the same way about Mariana.

She regretted that she would never have the same relationship with Marc that Mariana shared with Daniel. Lauren watched the couple across from her and she saw Mariana reach out and take Daniel's hand into her own. Lauren realized that she shared the same type of camaraderie with Marc but not the intimacy that would allow her to hold his hand at a restaurant.

Lauren felt her life was full of 'if onlys'. If only Marc thought of her as a woman, not a running companion. If only Marc was not dating Sylvia. If only Marc didn't think she was dating Jim. If only. Lauren let out a sigh.

"Everything alright, Lauren?" Patrick asked.

Lauren mentally shook herself, trying to focus her attention on the dinner conversation around her. "Yes, I'm fine. I think I'm just a little tired from the trip down after a long day at work, that's all."

Patrick seemed to accept her explanation without questioning her further. "Fridays can be tough." A short time later the bill arrived and the two men split the cost of the dinner between them and the group headed for the door.

Lauren watched as Daniel said goodbye to Mariana and she wished again that she would one day have a similar relationship with Marc. Lauren had to mentally shake herself. *I have to be realistic and not daydream about the impossible,* she thought to herself. She struggled to keep from crying, but a single lone tear escaped and trickled down her cheek. Luckily she was able to brush it away without any of the other three noticing.

Saturday morning was clear and crisp, unlike other days that Lauren had experienced in Los Angeles. Mariana had tried to tell her that the worst smog months were towards the end of the summer and Lauren had to agree if this morning was any indicator.

"It really is amazing during the winter months," Mariana said as they sipped their early morning tea outside by the pool. Lauren marveled at the differences between the two cities. In Santa Barbara she ran alongside the Pacific ocean every day. The ocean was accessible in Los Angeles as well, but Lauren found that most people enjoyed the water found inside their own swimming pools rather than making their way towards the waterfront.

Lauren had tried to run earlier in the morning, but had felt uncomfortable running along the sidewalks that bordered the manicured lawns in Westwood. Apparently the saying that 'no one walks in LA' also applied to running. When she'd made a comment to her friend about the lack of runners Mariana had laughed and told her that many people used local gyms for both working out and socializing.

As Mariana placed her cup on the table she asked, "So, are you ready to tell me what's going on?" It didn't take Lauren long to fill Mariana in on the caseload she was working on at her office and the different offers she'd received from the two law schools. It was harder for her to discuss Marc so she avoided speaking of him altogether.

"Lauren, you're not fooling me. There's more to this than work and law school. Now tell me, who is he? And don't tell me Jim because I won't buy it for a minute."

Lauren laughed self-consciously. "What makes you think it doesn't have anything to do with Jim?" she asked to avoid the direct question of her friend.

"Look, honey...I've been dating Daniel for several months now and I'm crazy about him. How many months have you been dating Jim?" and without waiting for Lauren to answer, Mariana continued, "I've never seen you even once get emotional about Jim and I can't imagine anything that could have happened to have you starting now."

Lauren sighed. "You're right. I don't get emotional over Jim. That's why we ended our dating relationship."

"Good for you. I never understood why you dated him in the first place."

"Mariana!"

"Well, it's true. Now tell me, who is he?"

Lauren didn't know how to avoid her friend's probing questions any longer. It only took a few minutes to tell her friend about the handsome attorney that was working at the firm.

"Wait a minute. You mean this is the guy you told me you've been running with?" Mariana asked.

"Yes, that's the one."

"You never told me he was good looking. You made it sound like he was just one of the guys from the office," Lauren's friend scolded playfully.

"How could I have told you something that I didn't know myself?"

"You mean you didn't realize that Mr. Harland was so dishy when you first met him?" Mariana teased.

"No... I mean yes, I knew how good looking he was, but Mariana, I didn't realize that I was in love with him."

Mariana poured more tea for both of them. "Ah...love. This is more serious than I thought. Well, have you told him yet?"

"Mariana!"

"Well, have you?"

"I can't tell him that!"

"Why not?"

"Well...well..." Lauren started to sputter. "It's just that he's dating this other woman..."

"Is he married?"

"No."

"Then tell him."

"He's leaving the firm after the trial and probably coming to Los Angeles."

"So? Tell him."

"He thinks I'm dating Jim."

"So tell him you're not and then tell him you love him."

"It's not that easy," Lauren persisted.

Mariana let out a sigh. "Sure it is. You've got nothing to lose. What's the worst thing that can happen?"

"He can laugh in my face and I'll never be able to look at him again."

"Or you end up together and make lots of babies happily ever after," Mariana continued. "Sounds like enough of a reason to tell him."

Lauren started to laugh. "You make it sound so easy but really it's not. What about you and Daniel? Was it that easy?"

Mariana's expression changed at the mention of Daniel's name. Yup, Mariana is definitely in love, Lauren thought. "Well, I accidentally banged his grocery cart with mine at the supermarket and it was love at first sight," Mariana replied. "It didn't take long before we realized that we were perfect for each other."

Lauren took a sip of her coffee. Too bad it wasn't that easy for her. She could remember seeing Marc on the beach that first day, with the wind blowing his hair and rippling his shirt against his firm stomach. She could remember how the sight of him had made her feel. Was that love at first sight or only lust at first sight? Lauren wondered. Several months ago she would have said it was impossible to fall in love at first sight, but now she didn't know.

"Oh, why does life have to be so hard?" Lauren groaned.

"I'm telling you. Talk to him and I bet you'll find out it wasn't hard at all."

Lauren wished that it could be so easy. It was great that her friend thought it was, but she knew better. Fairy tales happened in books, not real life.

"Come on, get dressed. We're going shopping," Mariana said as she jumped to her feet and pulled Lauren off of her chair. "I found the greatest place in the garment district downtown."

"I don't know, Mariana. I'm supposed to be saving for school, remember?"

"Oh come on. You know what they say...When the going gets tough, the tough go shopping." Mariana pushed her friend towards the bathroom. "You've got half an hour to get ready."

Lauren enjoyed shopping with her friend. Mariana was more flamboyant and pushed Lauren to try on a variety of clothes. "This reminds me of playing dress-up as a kid." Lauren laughed as her friend pushed her towards the dressing room with a teal colored dress with feather trim around the cuffs and the neckline.

When Lauren emerged from the dressing room she was laughing with feathers wisping around her face. "I think it's me. What do you think?" she asked jokingly.

Mariana stepped back in mock seriousness, appraising the tight fitting dress that complimented her friends figure surprisingly well. "Daahling... it's you, really." Mariana dropped the haughty accent and asked seriously. "How come you can take even the most ghastly dress and make it look good? It's not fair." Mariana pouted playfully.

"Me? Look at what you're wearing." Mariana looked down at the cream chiffon A-line dress that she had on and started to laugh. Lauren thought all the wispy layers to the dress made her friend look like an angel. "All you're missing is the wings."

"So, does that mean we should buy these?" Mariana asked.

"No! Look at all the bags we've already collected," Lauren said, pointing to the dressing room floor. "I wouldn't have any place to wear this anyway."

Mariana watched her friend walk back into the dressing room and pull the curtain across the entrance. She hoped Lauren would tell Marc how she felt about him. Her friend deserved the type of happiness that she had with Daniel.

Mariana didn't know Marc, but she knew her friend Lauren. Most of the men at the university were attracted to Lauren and she never seemed to notice. The way her friend had buried herself in her books she probably never actually noticed her admirers. Mariana doubted that Marc Harland was as immune to Lauren as she thought.

Lauren was having a wonderful weekend. After their shopping expedition, the two women had enjoyed lunch at a sidewalk cafe. Later in the afternoon they'd met up with Daniel and spent the evening in Westwood, watched the premier of a play at one of the large flashy theaters and attended the after-party at a trendy local restaurant.

On Sunday the three of them had enjoyed a final meal together before Lauren started her drive back to Santa Barbara. As she hugged her friend goodbye she thanked her. "This was a perfect weekend. Thanks for everything."

As Mariana hugged her friend in return she urged Lauren to talk to Marc. "What's the worst that can happen?"

Lauren started the drive back to Santa Barbara and tried to think of the various ways that she could talk to Marc.

Maybe her friend was right. She had everything to gain and nothing to lose. "Nothing except my dignity," Lauren thought to herself. "The worst that can happen is that I humiliate myself."

Lauren decided that she would talk to Marc but not when they were out running. If they were running she wouldn't be able to give the conversation enough attention. Also, if their talk went badly she would still have to get back to her apartment, presumably running the distance with Marc.

Lauren decided the best place would be at lunch or dinner in a public restaurant. She thought about inviting him over for dinner but was nervous that her home could be the most humiliating location if the talk did not go well. At least a public place like a restaurant could be both public and private and would allow for an easy escape if necessary.

Working through the details in her mind as she drove caused all of Lauren's uneasiness that had dissipated during her weekend to resurface. *Mariana is right,* Lauren thought as she tried to calm her fluttering nerves.

As Lauren drove from Summerland to Montecito to Santa Barbara her feelings of apprehension grew. *I have nothing to lose and everything to gain,* Lauren kept repeating to herself as she drove.

Lauren was thankful when she turned down the street that led to her apartment. She parked her car, collected her bags and walked up to her front door and let herself in. Buster was quick to come running and he purred his welcome as she approached. As she walked inside her apartment she dropped her bags at the entranceway and sat down on the couch. Buster quickly jumped up and joined her, curling into a purring ball in her lap. Lauren stroked her furry friend and could feel the apprehension and tension slowly fade again.

Lauren slept on and off during the night and was apprehensive again when she met Marc for their run the next morning. Marc asked her about her weekend and filled her in on the details of his own. Lauren thought it sounded like he even missed her while she was gone. The thought gave her hope and enough courage to ask if Marc wanted to have lunch with her. It was time for Lauren to take the bull by the horns.

"That sounds great. Any idea where you want to go?"

Lauren felt the uneasiness return. She'd been concentrating so hard on asking him that she hadn't thought about location. "I don't know. Is there anywhere you want to go?" Lauren tried to think of a location that would allow them some privacy. She could feel her palms getting sweaty.

"Why don't we see what kind of food sounds appealing and play it by ear," Marc responded casually. "We can decide when we get ready to go."

"Alright. Is noon good for you?"

"Should be."

"Alright, I'll see you then," Lauren answered. She could feel her knees getting weak and was thankful that she was able to head towards her apartment, away from Marc. She tried to take several deep breaths of air to soothe her nerves.

A short time later Lauren was showered and changed and ready to head for her office. Her resolve from the weekend seemed to be slipping away, but she'd made the first step. Lunch. Hopefully it would go well. Lauren prayed that it would.

Lauren tried to rehearse her upcoming conversation with Marc as she walked to work. If everything didn't go well she hoped she could retain some of her dignity. Lauren felt it was risky to approach this right before the start of the case, but she had to resolve the situation sooner rather than later. She was tired of running from her feelings.

As Lauren pushed open the doors to the law firm she almost ran into Sylvia as the young woman was leaving the firm. Sylvia's presence reminded Lauren that her conversation with Marc may be harder than she'd thought.

"Oh, good morning, Lauren. How are you?"

"Fine, Sylvia. What brings you here?" Lauren asked before she realized that the answer would probably be Marc, an answer she didn't want to hear.

"Oh, just some business. Marc and I are looking for a house together and I needed to get his signature before I could submit an offer."

Lauren felt a knife turn in her stomach and she felt like she was going to be sick. Marc. A house. With Sylvia. Lauren could feel the color draining from her face.

"But... but I thought he was leaving after the Consumer Energy case?"

"Oh. Didn't he tell you? He's decided to stay in Santa Barbara. Isn't that great?" Sylvia asked.

"Yeah, that's great," Lauren said quietly in reply. "If you'll excuse me..."

"Sure. Good seeing you, Lauren. Bye." Sylvia answered as Lauren felt her world crumbling around her. As she watched the door shut behind the other woman Lauren realized what a fool she'd been. Marc hadn't even told her he was going to be staying in Santa Barbara after the trial. Obviously he didn't have any feelings for her if he didn't even share that information with her. And she'd thought they were at least friends. But he hadn't even discussed this with her. *Some friendship.*

Lauren hurried towards her office and shut the door. At least she'd been saved from completely humiliating herself at lunch later that day. Lunch. How would she ever make it through? Lauren straightened and resolved to be strong. She was a professional and she would treat Marc as a colleague, nothing more.

As she looked around her office she realized that Marc seemed to be around her everywhere. There were several notes on the top of her desk that pertained to the upcoming case.

Marc's bold handwriting was only one reminder. Lauren couldn't walk around the firm offices without remembering a time that she'd shared with Marc in what seemed like every corner.

Lauren reached inside one of her desk drawers and pulled out the two packets for law school. It appeared there was only one choice now.

CHAPTER NINE

Marc came into Lauren's office late in the morning. She wondered if he would tell her he that he'd decided to stay at the firm when they were at lunch. It didn't matter. Lauren's world had been shattered when she had spoken to Sylvia earlier that morning.

Lauren pulled out the two law school packets and filled in the paperwork to accept the financial package from the university in Michigan. She hoped to feel excited about her decision, but all she felt was sadness as she sealed the envelope and affixed the stamp.

Next she filled in the paperwork to decline the Santa Barbara University offer. As she sealed the second envelope she felt she was sealing the end of her relationship with Marc. *Who am I kidding?* Lauren asked herself. She reminded herself that she didn't have a relationship with Marc. It was better to leave for Michigan. Staying at the firm would be too difficult. Working with Marc every day knowing he was sharing a home with Sylvia would be more than she could bear.

The kisses they'd shared must have meant nothing to Marc even though they had shaken Lauren's world.

Shortly before noon, Marc entered her office. "Ready for lunch?" he asked casually.

"Sure. Are you hungry for anything in particular?" Lauren replied, trying to sound light and carefree even though her heart ached.

They chose an Italian restaurant that they'd been to several times before located down the street from the firm.

On the elevator heading down to the first floor of the office building, Lauren remembered the envelopes on the corner of her desk. She scolded herself inwardly for forgetting the envelopes for law school. After all, law school was the only future she had. She would have to remember to mail the two envelopes later that afternoon.

Marc seemed relaxed and comfortable as they were seated at the table. "Have you decided what you would like to get? I was thinking we could split a pizza if you'd like."

"That sounds good," Lauren replied, thankful she wouldn't have to make a decision. It was hard to focus on the menu in front of her and she hoped she would be able to eat enough food once it had arrived to avoid arousing suspicion. She didn't feel much like eating.

"What types of toppings would you like on the pizza?" Marc asked, breaking through her thoughts.

"What?... Oh, toppings. I don't care. Anything but anchovies."

Marc laughed. "No problem," he answered as he closed his menu. As the waiter approached, Marc ordered a pepperoni and olive pizza, along with a Caesar salad and two large ice teas.

She'd grown accustomed to Marc in her life and now she didn't know how she would live without him.

After the waiter delivered their drinks, Marc turned to Lauren. "I'm glad we had the chance to have lunch today. I have some good news I would like to share with you."

Lauren picked up a freshly baked roll from the basket the waiter had brought with their drinks and focused her attention on buttering it meticulously.

"I wanted to let you know that I'm considering staying with the firm. Leo and I are still working out the details, so I didn't want to mention it sooner, but it looks like we're getting close to an agreement."

Marc looked happy as he told her about his plans. Lauren felt like she'd been kicked in the stomach. Marc had just confirmed the conversation Lauren had had with Sylvia earlier that morning. Marc had decided to stay in Santa Barbara. Marc had decided to stay because of Sylvia. There was no future for Lauren in Marc's life. There was no future for Lauren in Santa Barbara.

"That's great, Marc," Lauren replied carefully. "I have some news of my own. I've decided to attend the University in Michigan this coming semester."

Marc looked stunned. Lauren saw several emotions cross over his face before he replied. His face looked stricken with dismay. Lauren couldn't understand why her decision would impact him that way. It was obvious to Lauren that she was nothing more than a running companion and work colleague to Marc.

Marc was slow to respond. "Congratulations, Lauren. But I thought you would be staying in Santa Barbara to attend the law program here. I know Leo was hoping you would stay."

Lauren noticed that he didn't say that he'd hoped she would stay. Obviously she misinterpreted Marc's reaction to her announcement. He was only concerned that Leo would be disappointed.

The waiter approached their table and Lauren waited to reply until after he'd delivered their salads. "I haven't told Leo yet. I just made the decision this morning," Lauren replied. "I would appreciate it if you didn't say anything before I've had a chance to let him know about my decision."

"No problem. What does Jim have to say about Michigan? I don't see him as the type that would relish a move." Marc's voice sounded businesslike.

"Actually, Jim and I are no longer seeing each other," Lauren said quietly. She'd certainly hoped to let Marc know about the end of her relationship with Jim under different circumstances. Lauren focused her attention on the salad in front of her.

Marc's expression showed a quick glimpse of relief and understanding before his businesslike expression returned. Lauren took a bite of her salad and didn't see the change in Marc's expression.

Lauren let out a sigh. At least she would be able to be near her parents while she attended law school in Michigan. She hoped that over time the pain she felt inside would subside.

"Are you looking forward to the polo match this weekend?" Marc asked casually as he put a piece of pizza on his plate.

The polo match! Lauren had forgotten all about the upcoming weekend. "I don't know much about polo, but I think it will be fun." Inwardly Lauren wished there would be a way to excuse herself from the event. Attending the polo match with Marc would be difficult, especially with Leo and Lily coming along.

Their ongoing conversation centered on the game of polo and their morning run the next day. Marc explained some of the basics of a polo match, outlining that the game was played on a large grass field, several times larger than a football field. He also said that the match was broken down into several time periods, referred to as chukkers. Lauren was familiar with the innings of a baseball game and the quarters for basketball and football, but chukkers was a term she'd never heard.

Somehow Lauren managed to make it through the remainder of the lunch without revealing her inner turmoil. Listening to Marc's voice explaining the components of polo reminded her of the afternoon they went sailing and she felt a pain that ripped her heart in two.

After they returned to the firm, Lauren excused herself and hurried to her office. Having lunch with Marc had taken more energy out of her than she thought.

During the next several days, meeting Marc to go running was bittersweet to Lauren. She reveled in their time together, but there was always an inner voice reminding her that there could never be anything more between the two of them.

"Is everything alright, Lauren?" Marc asked as they circled around the bird sanctuary the following day. Marc had been watching Lauren closely for the last several days and he believed the breakup between Lauren and Jim was more devastating to Lauren than he'd first thought or wanted to believe. She'd seemed so listless the past few days.

"Yeah, I'm fine," Lauren said breathlessly. It was the same response she'd given him the other times he'd asked. Marc was trying to be patient, but he was feeling frustrated.

"I'll race you around the perimeter of the sanctuary," Marc said playfully, trying to involve Lauren with the present activity, trying to pull her out of the cocoon she seemed to have wrapped around herself.

Lauren tried to sound cheerful as she agreed to the race. The last several days had been very difficult for her. The hours around Marc at the firm were hard, but Lauren found that their morning runs together were particularly painful. The two of them were more playful and relaxed while they were running than the atmosphere at the firm allowed.

Lauren saw the way that Marc was looking at her lately and she wished that she could be far away from his sympathy. He'd been understanding and had tried hard to include her in a variety of activities but Lauren had been hesitant to join him.

Marc had invited her sailing again and suggested touring the wine country located around Santa Barbara, but Lauren had turned him down each time. She was afraid it would be too difficult to be around him. But now, racing after him around the sanctuary, Lauren was beginning to wonder. Maybe it would be better to enjoy the next several weeks they would be able to share together before Marc moved in with Sylvia. Lauren was sure the other woman would be possessive and would put a stop to their morning runs. Lauren was actually surprised that Sylvia hadn't put a stop to her daily rendezvous with Marc already.

When Lauren caught up to Marc she was out of breath and she found herself laughing between gasps for air. "That wasn't fair! You had a head start." Lauren's green eyes sparkled as she connected with the dark blue of Marc's gaze and she hoped the love she felt for him wasn't too evident. "I'm thirsty. Do you want to get some freshly squeezed punch at the juice bar down the street?" she asked to cover up the sudden awkwardness she felt.

"Sure, that sounds great." Marc looked into Lauren's eyes and hoped that the Lauren he'd gotten to know over the past several months was back. The magical expression he saw now on her face was like so many others he'd seen before the beginning of this week.

Marc tried to curb the anger he felt towards Jim Adamson. It was apparent to Marc that Jim was at the root of Lauren's despair. He hated the idea of Lauren being hurt, especially by the likes of Jim Adamson.

The juice bar located along Cabrillo Boulevard had a variety of tropical concoctions that were meant to be both healthy and refreshing. They both ordered a blend of guava, pineapple and passion fruit juices. Lauren thought the pale pink of their drinks looked like a sunset in a glass.

Marc turned towards Lauren and lifted his drink. "Cheers," he said. Lauren raised her glass in response and the two glasses sounded musical as they made contact. "Cheers," Lauren echoed and she took a sip.

"Well, the polo match is only a few days away," Marc said in a relaxed tone. "It looks like Leo and I are about to reach an agreement. What did Leo say when you told him you would be leaving the firm?"

Lauren could feel her cheeks warm with a blush. "Actually, I haven't told him yet." Lauren mentally kicked herself. She was reminded by Marc's question that the envelope to accept the position in the Michigan school was still on the corner of her desk, unmailed.

Lauren also realized that she needed to call her parents and let them know about her decision. The few times she'd thought to call it was too late in the evening due to the time difference. Maybe she would have time to connect with her mother before she left for work that morning.

It didn't take Lauren long to get ready in the morning after her morning run. As she walked into her living room she was reminded to call her mother when she saw the telephone.

Lauren was hesitant to pick up the phone. Normally Lauren loved the calls she shared with her parents, but something was holding her back from making this call.

Lauren let the phone ring seven times before replacing the receiver back on the base of the phone. She looked at her watch. It was eight o'clock which meant that it was eleven in the morning in Michigan. Her father would be at the small family grocery store he'd run for the last twenty years. It was likely that her mother was also at the store or running errands, having recently retired from her secretarial position.

Lauren made a mental note to herself as she picked up her briefcase and purse to call her parents later in the day when she had a break at work and she headed towards her front door.

Later that morning, when Lauren was coming out of the law library she ran into Leo in the hall.

"Good, good, Lauren. I've found you. The big polo match is tomorrow. Are you ready? It should prove to be a fascinating game."

"I'm looking forward to the match, Leo," Lauren said, trying to sound enthusiastic. "Marc explained some of the basics of the game."

Leo chuckled. "We'll have you an expert in no time. If you attack polo the same way you do a case it won't be much time at all."

Lauren awoke the next morning dreading the day in front of her. Part of her ached to be as close to Marc as possible, another part of her felt so much pain it was almost too much to bear.

She stood in front of her closet trying to decide what to wear. Lauren hadn't thought to inquire about the appropriate attire. She knew that polo was traditionally viewed as a formal and serious sport which mandated an audience dressed in style. Santa Barbara was known for its relaxed attitude and Lauren felt confident that the attire to the match would be varied.

Lauren finally selected a green sundress with straps that crisscrossed across her back and a large taupe colored cardigan sweater to put on in case the weather turned cool. She slipped on a pair of open leather sandals and looked into the long mirror on the back of her bedroom door.

She felt comfortable with the end result as she gazed at her reflection. Her auburn hair looked dark and rich against the neutral taupe color of her sweater and the green of the sundress deepened the color of her eyes.

As she was transferring several items into a small purse, her telephone rang. Lauren looked at her watch as she walked over to the phone. It was still early in the morning, almost too early to expect a call from anyone. Lauren felt a wave of panic as she picked up the phone.

"Lauren, honey?" Lauren heard her mother's voice over the receiver of the phone and she felt her heartbeat begin to quicken.

"Mom, is everything alright?" she asked hastily. "Is Dad ok?"

"We're both fine, honey. We've just had a devil of a time trying to reach you and I thought if I called early enough I might actually catch you. Did you get my messages?"

Lauren let out a sigh of relief. "Yeah, Mom. I tried calling you back, but I didn't get an answer," she replied. "I have some news I wanted to share with you."

"Oh, that's great dear. Your father and I have something to share with you as well. You first, Lauren."

She took a deep breath. "Well, I wanted to let you know that I've decided to attend school in Michigan. I'll be moving back in several months."

"But honey, we thought you were happy in Santa Barbara. I guess your father and I just assumed you would be staying there once you'd heard there was no significant difference in the financial aid programs."

Lauren felt a wave of pain grip her heart. If it hadn't been for Marc Harland she would have loved to stay in Santa Barbara, but now she needed to run from the memories around her. Lauren tried to push the pain aside and listen to her mother.

"If that's what you want, Lauren, then I'm happy for you. We just didn't expect you to be moving back."

Lauren thought her mother sounded flustered. "Mom, don't you want me to move home?"

"Of course, dear... it's just...well... Here, talk to your father." Lauren was perplexed by her mother's reaction. She'd thought Helen Evans would be thrilled to hear her news. The one thought that had helped her make it through the past few days was knowing that her parents would be happy with her decision. She thought being with them would help ease the pain she felt inside.

Lauren could hear her parents muffled voices in the background as her mother handed the phone to her father. "Lauren..." the deep tone of her father, Steven Evans, boomed in her ear.

"Hi, Dad. How are you?" Lauren asked as she shook her head. She was perplexed. Her father should have been at the store by this time on a Saturday morning.

"I'm fine, honey. Just fine. Your mother tells me you've decided to attend school in Michigan. I don't know how to tell you this, so I'm just going to come out and say it. Lauren, your mother and I won't be here."

Lauren felt her knees go weak and she was afraid to stand for fear her legs would give out altogether. She slipped into the chair beside the phone table. "Wh..What do you mean you won't be there? Where are you going?" Lauren asked in a shaky voice.

"Lauren, your mother and I have been trying to reach you for a while now. We received an offer for the store that we felt we couldn't turn down. You know how it's been lately with the larger food stores coming into the area. We decided we wanted to enjoy ourselves. We've worked hard for so long it's time to have some fun."

Lauren was having trouble focusing. What was her father trying to tell her? Her mind was a blur. "Where are you going to live if you're not going to be in Michigan, Dad?"

"Well, Lauren, your mother and I have always wanted to travel. We've always wanted to see the country, but with the store, we've never been able to get away." Lauren could hear the excitement in her father's voice. He sounded like a kid as he continued. "Lauren, your mother and I have bought an R.V. and we're planning on travelling around the country. We're going to start on the Interstate and see where we end up."

"But, Dad, what about the house?" Lauren felt like she was talking to a stranger. This didn't sound like her father, the man who had always seemed so tired after long hours in the store. The man on the other end seemed years younger than the man she knew.

"Actually, Lauren, we're selling the house too."

"Isn't this rather sudden, Dad?" Lauren asked, trying to make sense of the situation.

"Lauren, I know this must be difficult for you..."

That's a slight understatement, Lauren thought sarcastically to herself as her father continued. "Your Mother and I have been thinking about what we would like to do when we retire for some time. The sale of the store was rather quick, but it really is something that we've thought about for some time now. I hope you understand, honey."

Her parent's sudden news was beginning to sink into Lauren's shell shocked brain. The news that her parents weren't going to be in Michigan had torn the safety net of family away from her.

Lauren felt a wave of despair take over her. She felt like she no longer had a home: not in Santa Barbara and not in Michigan.

"Don't worry, honey. We can make California our first stop if you'd like. We'd love to see where you've been living for the last several years."

Lauren tried to concentrate on the conversation with her parents. She tried hard to feel happy for them. She tried not to focus on her own problems. Shortly after they dropped their bombshell, Lauren's parents bid her farewell and Lauren replaced the phone receiver in the cradle. She sat and stared at the phone for several minutes after the call had ended.

The knock on her front door startled her. She looked at her watch as she jumped up and realized it was no longer early. She opened the door and found Marc on her doorstep. Her heart caught in her throat as she let him into her apartment.

His large frame filled the doorway as he entered. He was dressed in a navy blue sweater and khaki denim pants. The sight of him made Lauren catch her breath. She could feel her pulse quicken and as he brushed by her to enter the room, she could feel her body start to tingle.

"You look lovely today, Lauren," Marc said as he entered the room. The compliment caught Lauren off guard. As she thanked him she realized that it was going to be a long, painful day.

"I told Leo and Lily that we would meet them at the polo field. Are you ready to go?"

"Sure, just let me get my purse and keys and I'll be ready," Lauren replied and they headed for the door.

Marc drove his black Porsche down the road that led towards the Santa Barbara Polo and Racquet Club. The field was located several miles from Lauren's apartment and they had filled the time with casual conversation.

Marc had informed Lauren that Leo and Lily would be meeting them at the field before they had started the drive from her apartment. As Marc made the left hand turn that brought them onto the grounds of the club, Lauren caught her breath.

The field was magnificent. The narrow lane that led them down the center of the grounds was tree-lined and flanked by several white buildings with hunter green trim. If it hadn't been for the Santa Ynez mountains that bordered the club, Lauren would have felt like she was in Kentucky.

To the left of the driveway was a corral area used for pacing the horses. On the right side of the drive was a large playing field.

"Impressive, isn't it?" Marc asked as he pulled his car onto a portion of the grass bordering the field.

"It's huge," Lauren replied in awe.

"The length of the field is about the size of three football fields."

"I had no idea it would be so large a playing area."

"Well, with eight horses chasing a little white ball at high speed, you need a lot of room," Marc answered with a twinkle in his eye.

Lauren looked around her. The area was swarming with people, horses, and trailers. Lauren felt overwhelmed. "If there are only eight horses on the field, why are there so many here?" Lauren was able to count twenty horses from her vantage point and she was sure there were more.

Marc laughed as he replied, "The horses are traded out during the game so they aren't overtired. Generally a horse is never used for more than two chukkers during a match and never consecutively. With a match consisting of six chukkers, it's conceivable that a rider may use six different horses during one match."

"That's amazing. I had no idea." Lauren was afraid she was sounding like a broken record. The view in front of her had caught her off guard. As she continued to look around her, one of the riders led a horse by Marc's car. The horse was elaborately prepared for the game ahead. Lauren was enthralled with the preparation. The horse's tail had been carefully braided and the shins wrapped. The rider himself appeared to have taken great care with his own preparation. He was wearing a colored jersey and thick leather pads that ran the length of his boots and covered his knees. He was also carrying a mallet made out of bamboo that he'd draped casually over his shoulder. There was a number on the sleeve of his shirt and as he passed, she could see the same number across the back of the shirt.

Lauren was excited about the game. The apprehension she'd been feeling from the news of her parents' move and her feelings towards Marc and Sylvia were temporarily gone. She felt caught up in the excitement around her.

"Come on, let's walk around the grounds," Marc said as he opened the driver side door. Lauren opened her own car door and followed.

There were crowds of people milling around. Lauren felt that there were people or horses everywhere. Marc must have sensed her fear of separation because he reached out and took her hand and helped lead her through the mass.

It didn't take Marc long to make his way through the crowd towards one of the white buildings they'd driven by when they'd first arrived. Lauren realized that it was a concession stand serving a variety of foods and beverages.

"What would you like to drink?" Marc asked over the noise of the crowd around them. Lauren struggled to see the board in front of her that listed the drinks available. "What are you going to have?" she asked Marc.

"I think I'll have a cold beer."

"I'll have one, too," Lauren called back to Marc. It wasn't what she normally would have chosen to drink but it was a warm afternoon and a beer would be refreshing. She also hoped the alcohol would help soothe her ruffled emotions.

Within minutes Marc was handing her a plastic glass filled with ice cold amber liquid. The beer tasted slightly bitter as she took a sip, but it was cool and refreshing.

"Come on, let's try to move away from this crowd. Would you like to see the horses, Lauren?"

"Actually, it's 'would you like to see the ponies, Lauren,'" Leo's voice boomed from behind them. Lauren and Marc both turned towards the older man. Leo was with his wife, Lily, who looked radiant. Lauren felt a wave of envy wash over her as she looked at the couple. She'd hoped that one day she and Marc would be like the two standing in front of them. She sighed to herself as she tried to focus on the conversation the two men were having.

"Marcus," Leo boomed, getting everyone's attention within the radius around them.

"Yes, sir!" Marc grinned as he replied.

"Marcus," Leo repeated a slight fraction softer than before. "They are ponies, Polo p-o-n-i-e-s," he said, drawing out the syllables as he spoke. Leo was in a good mood and he laughed as he reached out and patted Marc on the back. "Come with me for a minute. I have something I'd like to discuss with you." Leo turned toward Lily and Lauren. "Please excuse us. We won't be long."

Lauren watched the two men walk off towards the corral area. Marc was taller and younger than Leo, but there was a bond between the two men. Lauren could sense a fraternity among men at the firm. As she turned towards Lily she felt like it was a fraternity she would never be able to join, never be able to be part of.

"Lauren, my dear. How are you?" Lily asked as they walked towards a bench that was under a tree. "Why don't we sit in the shade over here and catch up on all the gossip."

Lauren smiled as she sat down. For all her efforts at the firm, here she was sitting, the men off on their own and the women together. Lauren adored Lily and she enjoyed the time she was able to spend with the older woman. It didn't bother her much that she had been dismissed from the two men's conversation. She looked out towards the corral and her eyes locked with Marc's as Leo talked with him and Lauren felt connected to the two men even though she wasn't included in their conversation.

Lauren broke her gaze with Marc and turned toward Lily. "I'm sorry, Lily, what did you just say?"

"Oh, my dear, that's perfectly alright. I was just saying how happy Leo is that Marc has decided to stay at the firm. He is a very talented young man."

"Yes, yes he is," Lauren replied wistfully, her voice full of love and pride for the man she knew. She tried to bury the pain she felt inside, knowing that he loved another woman.

Lily reached out and patted Lauren's hand. "Love is wonderful, dear. Look, it's made a different man out of Marc Harland. In many ways I believe his life was not complete. Even though he was very successful when I first met him, he seemed to be missing something. That something was love."

Lauren felt her throat constrict as she listened to Lily. She too had noticed a change in Marc over the past several months. She'd been a fool to think that the change had anything to do with the two of them. It was now obvious to

Lauren that the change in Marc had been brought about by Sylvia. Lauren felt like a fool.

"Well, that didn't take too long, now did it?" Leo boomed in Lauren's ear. The two men approached the bench and joined the two women. "Sorry about that, but Marc and I just had a few details to work out. It looks like we've come to an agreement on Marc staying with the firm. I'd like to present to you the newest partner of Whitman, Hawkins & Smythe."

Partner! Lauren had never expected that Marc would be made a partner. It was customary to join the firm as an associate and work up to the level of partner.

"Congratulations, Marc," Lauren said, pride reflected in her voice. It was too bad she wouldn't be able to share in his success. She would be gone from the firm soon.

"Good, good. That's all been worked out," Leo boomed. "I've reserved a table for us over on the other side of the concession stand. Let's enjoy a pleasant lunch before we make our way to the stands to observe the match."

They made their way over to the dining area. Lunch was exquisite. Lauren felt completely pampered from the beginning of the meal. The tablecloths and napkins were crisply starched and their waiter hovered around their table trying to anticipate their every need.

Lauren took a bite of her Waldorf salad as she listened to Leo discuss the strategy behind polo. Marc had been very knowledgeable when they had discussed the game prior to arriving at the polo field; however, Leo had years of experience with watching and as Lauren learned, playing the game.

"Oh, well, that was years ago." Leo had dismissed his playing casually.

"Dear, you were wonderful to watch," Lily replied as she turned toward Marc and Lauren. "Leo was pure poetry in motion when he was on the back of a pony. He developed quite a reputation for his skill before he retired from the game."

"Leo, I had no idea! What other secrets have you been hiding from us?" Lauren asked.

Leo laughed mysteriously as he replied, "Oh, lots of things... lots of things."

"Well, Lauren, my dear, you could say that it was a polo pony that brought Leo and I together. Isn't that right, darling?" Lily asked her adoring husband.

"Sure is." Leo leaned closer to the table as he recounted the events of many years ago. "It was a day very much like this one. A big match was going to be played and I was one of the players. I was sponsored by one of the club members, otherwise I would never have been able to afford to play."

"Polo can be very expensive," Lily interjected before her husband continued.

"That's right. The club member, his name was George, had several new ponies that he wanted me to try out. One in particular was very feisty."

"Skittish is more like it." Lily laughed.

"Actually, Lily is right. This one pony in particular was uncomfortable with all the commotion of the crowds and the other horses. George's trainer was having a devil of a time trying to control him."

"He was a beautiful animal," Lily said quietly as she patted her husband's hand.

"Anyway, right about this time, while the trainer and I were trying to control the pony, a beautiful woman wearing a white linen dress came strolling by. I thought she was a vision before my eyes. I'd never seen a woman who looked so beautiful," Leo said as he took his wife's hand into his own from across the table.

"Well, I must have loosened my grip on the reins because at that moment the pony decided to rear up on his hind legs, scaring poor Lily half to death."

"All I could see were horse hooves and metal horse shoes," Lily added.

"It was all I could do to hand the pony over to the trainer, but within moments I was able to be at Lily's side and make sure she was alright."

"And he's been at my side ever since," Lily concluded the story. Lauren watched the older woman squeeze the hand of her husband. They were perfect, even after all of the years they'd been married. Lauren could feel the tears welling up in her eyes and she swallowed hard to remove the tightness in her throat.

"Well, shall we move over to the grandstands and get ready for the match?" Leo asked cheerfully. Within minutes they were all seated on the border of the great expanse of the playing field.

There were a few spectators on the other side of the field and they looked like small miniatures because of the distance between them. Lauren was awed by the sheer size of the field.

"Here, these ought to help," Leo said to Lauren as he handed her a pair of binoculars. "The trouble you'll have is keeping the horses in your sights. You might find it easier to get a sense of the game without the binoculars, but it can be fun to use them for part of the game."

Lauren noticed that Marc had been quiet during the story Leo and Lily had told over lunch. She'd caught him looking at her intently several times during lunch and it had made her feel uneasy. Luckily the game was about to start and the sooner it ended the sooner she could get back to her home and be alone away from Marc's dark looks.

Shortly after they'd been seated in the firm's private section of the grandstand, the ball was thrown in and the game began. The match was thrilling. Lauren felt herself being caught up with the excitement. Players called to each other over thundering horse hooves and the "thwack" of bamboo mallets connecting with a small bamboo ball to send it flying down the field could be heard from their seats. Divots of the field flew as pounds of horse and men followed in hot pursuit.

"Amongst all the commotion it really is a graceful game, don't you agree, Lauren?" Marc leaned over and whispered in her ear.

Lauren felt the warm breath of his voice caress her cool neck and she felt a shiver of excitement run through her body. No matter where Marc was she always felt aware of his strength and the smell of his masculine scent. She felt bound to him, trapped in a sensual world she had no desire to leave but a world she felt held no place for her.

Lauren felt her voice sounded groggy as she responded to Marc. "It's almost like ballet on horseback."

Marc's laughter rippled down her spine and she fought the urge to lean back and rest against his strong powerful legs. She wished he would wrap his arms around her and never let her go.

"I'd never thought about it that way." There was Marc's warm voice caressing her neck again. Lauren wondered what it would feel like to have him brush her hair to one side and kiss the exposed portion of her neck. Lauren suddenly understood why virgins surrendered their necks so willingly to vampires in the old black and white horror films she had watched as a teenager.

Luckily, the first chukker didn't last long and Lauren was able to excuse herself from the group. Marc gave her another one of his dark, questioning looks as she got up to leave and she joked about needing to powder her nose. As Lauren made her way past the concession stand she thought she needed more than a nose powdering. *More like a cold shower*, she thought wryly.

Lauren felt taut with emotion as she splashed cool water on her face. She held her hands under the steady stream of cool liquid flowing in front of her and she tried to push thoughts of Marc Harland away from her mind. She'd known today was going to be difficult, but she hadn't expected the sensual onslaught at being so near to him. She struggled with bittersweet emotions as she dried her face and hands. She looked at her reflection in the mirror and applied a little lipstick to her bare lips. She was stalling, taking extra care to smooth her hair and dress before she ventured back outside.

"Oh, there you are, Lauren. I was beginning to get worried," Marc said as she approached the firm's box.

"It's pretty crowded. I'm going to get a drink, does anybody want anything?" Lauren replied.

Lauren took Leo and Lily's order and she turned towards Marc. "Do you want anything?"

"I'll come with you."

"NO!... I mean, it's alright... really. I can manage," Lauren said hastily. She wanted as much distance between her and Marc as possible. The match had only begun and by every indication it was going to be a long day.

Lauren turned and started back towards the concession stand. She could feel Marc's eyes on her back as she made her way. She thought he might be following her, but she didn't dare look behind her. She increased her speed to try to put more distance between them.

"Lauren!" Marc called out to her and Lauren could feel the heat of his body next to hers. Within seconds he'd caught up to her and grabbed her wrist and pulled her towards him. His sudden pull on her arm threw their bodies together forcefully as she pivoted around to face him. She could feel the length of his body next to hers and she felt the muscles in her legs become weak as she molded herself to him. The sound of the crowd and the thundering horse hooves around her was replaced with the sound of her pounding heart.

Marc's mouth came down on hers with an intensity that matched her fantasies from moments before. Lauren returned Marc's kiss with all the love and passion she'd been trying to keep bottled inside her. She forgot about everything except the moment. She didn't realize that she had put her arms around his neck until she became conscious of his hair intertwined in her fingertips.

She could feel the hardness of his body against her and she never wanted to let go. But suddenly Marc was breaking away from her, his voice shaking slightly as he spoke.

"We've got to talk. Come with me." Marc grabbed her hand and pulled her through the crowds to the corral area on the other side of the lane. There was a musty smell of hay that greeted Lauren as Marc continued to pull her along towards one of the horse shelters. As they went inside, Lauren blinked, trying to focus from the sudden change in light of the bright afternoon sun to the shadows within the barn.

They didn't speak for several moments. Lauren looked around her, the stalls and equipment taking shape in front of her as her eyes adjusted to the light.

The barn was empty. The horses and trainers used a corral located by the playing field during a competition.

As Lauren's eyes adjusted she could see Marc's face clearly and she watched him prop himself against a bale of hay. He looked shaken and was beginning to breathe more normally.

"Are you leaving for Michigan because of Jim Adamson?" Marc asked abruptly.

Lauren took a deep breath. She remembered what her friend Mariana had said about telling Marc the truth. She let out a sigh before she said quietly. "No, I'm leaving because of you."

Marc looked stunned. "Me? I don't understand. Why? What have I done?"

"I can't bear the thought of you living with another woman, so I've decided to leave."

"What are you talking about?" Marc crossed the room quickly and took hold of both of her shoulders. Lauren wondered if he was going to start shaking the words out of her. "Or, should I ask, who are you talking about?"

Lauren felt embarrassed. She shouldn't have started this conversation but she had, and the words started to tumble out. "Sylvia. I ran into Sylvia the other day and she said you were looking for a house together and... and then you announced you were staying with the firm...and I couldn't stay here any longer... I thought my world was falling apart."

Marc started to laugh as he picked Lauren up and twirled her around. "Oh, Lauren, Lauren... I love you."

When Marc stopped swinging Lauren around and her feet were firmly planted on the ground, she still felt off balance. "What do you mean, you love me?"

"Lauren, I love you. That means I want to spend the rest of my life with you. I want to wake up with you every morning and go to sleep with you by my side every night. It means I want you to have our children. It means I want to be able to hold your hand when we are old and grey."

"But what about Sylvia? She said you were looking at houses together."

"I guess in a way she's right, but she's my realtor, nothing more. I've been looking for a house for us. You and me. A house I thought we could share for years to come."

"Why didn't you tell me?"

"Actually, I thought you were practically engaged to Jim. I was getting prepared for the battle to win you over. I was trying so hard to be patient, trying to let you make your own decisions about him and about me. I made arrangements with Leo to join the firm to give me the time I needed to win you over." Marc reached for Lauren's hands and held them tightly as he continued.

"I never expected you to break up with Jim and decide to leave the firm before I'd even had a chance to start. I felt like my world was falling apart."

Lauren felt laughter bubbling up inside her. "You felt like your world was falling apart! That's how I've felt all week. I thought I was going to have to watch you with another woman and that was more than I could possibly bear."

"Well, now you know what it was like watching you with Adamson. And then when I started seeing him around town with Sylvia, I thought he was a two timing snake. I couldn't bear the thought of you getting hurt by him."

"Jim is dating Sylvia?! He told me he was dating somebody, but he never told me it was her."

"You mean you knew?" Marc asked, stunned.

"Oh, Marc." Lauren reached up and cupped his face in her hands. "I realized, I think from the time I met you, that I wasn't in love with Jim. The only person I could think of was you. I ended it with Jim the day after you kissed me at the party. Jim never made me feel the way you did."

"So, it doesn't bother you that Jim is dating Sylvia?"

"Well, I'm surprised, but no, I'm not bothered just as long as Sylvia's not going after you! When Jim told me he was interested in dating another woman, I didn't realize it was Sylvia, but I was happy for him. He really is a wonderful person, just not the one I want."

"So, who do you want, Lauren?" Marc asked and he saw the answer in Lauren's eyes.

"Just in case there's a reasonable doubt, let me show you." Lauren felt like she'd found heaven as she reached for the man she loved. She could feel the ripple of muscle beneath his shirt as she rested her hands on his waist. She reached up to kiss him, tenderly at first and then the passion that flared inside her took over and she gasped for breath as she tugged on the bottom of his shirt and freed it from the waistband of his slacks.

Lauren slipped her hands under Marc's shirt and ran her fingertips across the firm muscles of his stomach up to his broad chest. Marc responded by pushing aside the wide shoulder strap of her sundress, pushing aside the cardigan as well, and he bent his head to kiss the soft flesh above her breast as he pushed the remaining fabric aside to expose her firm, taut nipple. Lauren arched her back and groaned as his lips and tongue teased her aching body.

Lauren undid the belt around Marc's waist, passion making her bolder than she ever would have imagined. Her fingers trembled as she struggled to accomplish her goal. Marc's strong arms went around the small of Lauren's back and he lowered her onto the hay-covered floor. Lauren watched as he undid the zipper that had been giving her trouble and she helped him free himself from his confining clothing.

"I love you, Lauren."

"I love you, too, Marc." That was all they said before their union was complete. Lauren could feel the vibrations of the thundering horse hooves from outside beneath her as the game continued, accenting the waves of passion that rode through her body.

Later, as they were lying with their bodies intertwined, Marc turned towards Lauren. "I'm sorry, this wasn't very romantic," he apologized while he plucked hay out of Lauren's hair.

"It was wonderful. You're wonderful." Lauren responded by nibbling his earlobe.

"Lauren, you never did answer me."

"What do you mean?"

"Lauren, my love, will you marry me? Will you have my children? Will you go to bed at night with me and wake up with me in the morning? Will you grow old with me?"

Lauren giggled. "Yes, Yes, YES!!! I thought you'd never ask!"

"I love you, Lauren, and I'm going to show you all over again just how much."

"Oh, no, Marc!"

"What, sweetheart?"

"Leo and Lily! Remember, we were getting them iced teas a long time ago, before you abducted me."

"You mean... before... I...seduced you..." Marc said between the kisses he planted on her face and neck. They felt the way Lauren had imagined they would.

"Yes! We have to get back. I'm sorry, darling, but..." Lauren looked at Marc mischievously. "I'll make it up to you later, I promise."

It didn't take them long to get dressed and laughingly brush hay off of their clothes. Within minutes, Marc was holding a tray of iced teas and they were heading back towards the grandstands.

"Marc, I'm so embarrassed. What are we going to tell them?" Lauren asked distressed.

"Why, the truth, of course."

"Marc! You wouldn't dare!" Lauren could feel her cheeks get warm at the thought.

"Leo, Lily, here are the iced teas. I'm sorry for the delay but Lauren and I had a few things we needed to discuss. I hope you don't mind that I stole her away for a little bit."

"No, not at all, dear," Lily replied. Lauren thought she had a knowing look in her eyes, but Lauren told herself she was just being paranoid.

"Actually, I have to apologize because we can't stay," Marc continued. "I have to take my fiancé to get a ring before she changes her mind on me." Lauren gasped.

"Well, I'll be damned. Good for you two," Leo said heartily.

"See, my dear, I told you love changes a man. Congratulations to both of you. Now, go ahead, get out of here. We certainly understand," Lily said. "Don't we, Leo?"

"Sure do, Lily," Leo replied as he squeezed his wife's hand.

Marc took Lauren's hand and led her towards his car. Lauren felt like she was walking a foot above the ground as she followed the man she loved.

CHAPTER ELEVEN

Marc unlocked the door of the car and helped Lauren inside. It didn't take him long to open his own door and climb in beside her.

Lauren was still feeling a little overwhelmed by the activities of the day. When had everything taken such a turn? Her love for Marc was making her feel drugged, with nothing clear except the strength of the man next to her.

Marc loved her! She wanted to open the car window and sing out to everyone around her.

Marc had gotten into the car, but he wasn't starting the engine.

"What's wrong?" Lauren asked tentatively.

Marc laughed. "Nothing, nothing at all. I was just thinking that my partnership at Whitman, Hawkins & Smythe is probably going to be the shortest partnership in history."

"What do you mean?" Lauren asked, the implications of his statement not fully penetrating through her whirling senses.

"I mean I'm going to be looking into passing the Michigan Bar exam. I certainly have no desire to be states away from my wife as she attends law school."

Michigan! Lauren had completely forgotten her decision to go away to school. This time it was Lauren's turn to laugh.

"Actually," she started playfully, "we can go to Michigan if you'd like, but I'd much prefer to stay here... that is if you want to."

Marc looked serious. "I will not have you give up law school. You've worked too long and hard to walk away from that now."

"Good, I'm glad you feel that way, because I have no intention of giving up my degree." Lauren giggled. "Actually, I haven't mailed the acceptance letter to Michigan yet and I haven't turned down Santa Barbara University either. Somehow I just didn't have the heart to mail in either envelope. It seemed so final," Lauren said in a serious tone. "Honestly, I would prefer to stay here."

Marc's reply was a kiss that made Lauren thankful she was sitting down.

As Marc drove the car off of the club grounds Lauren asked, "I wonder how the firm will feel about a husband and wife working together." Lauren liked the way that sounded.

"Don't worry, I'll just remind Leo about his first assistant."

"Lily?"

"Lily," Marc confirmed with a laugh.

The next several weeks flew by in a blur for Lauren. Marc had been actively involved with the Consumer Energy trial and everything seemed to be going well. Judge Rollins seemed tough but fair.

Lauren had quickly called her parents and told them the change in her plans. They were both very excited and responded that they were fueling up the camper and on their way. "There's no way my little girl is getting married before I meet the groom," Lauren's father had said. Lauren just smiled to herself. She knew her parents would like Marc as much as she loved him.

Next she had called Mariana. "Would you like to be my maid of honor?" Lauren had asked casually. Mariana had squealed.

Lauren spent her time running between the law firm and the courthouse during the day and a variety of other locations after work with Mariana trying to coordinate her wedding. Everything seemed white and bright. The fabric of her wedding dress, papers for the case and the walls of the courthouse all blended together and left Lauren feeling exhilarated.

Marc drove Lauren by the wonderful cottage they'd run by weeks earlier. Lauren giggled to herself as she thought back to the time that she'd thought Marc and Sylvia were going to be living there together. She was glad those days were behind her.

"Come on, I want to show you something." Marc pulled Lauren by the hand down the stone tiled driveway.

"Marc! We can't go down there, we're trespassing!" Lauren cried out as Marc incessantly pulled her forward. "Don't you know the law?" she joked as she realized he was not slowing down.

"Don't worry, I know the owner... I know he won't mind." Lauren allowed Marc to pull her towards the front door and her mouth dropped open as Marc reached inside his pocket and pulled out a key and fit it into the lock.

As Marc pushed open the front door he turned toward Lauren. "I know it's a little early, but I want to practice." And before Lauren realized what was happening, Marc leaned over, placed his right arm around her shoulders and quickly leaned down and slipped his left arm behind Lauren's legs and swung her up into his arms.

"Welcome home, darling," Marc said before he kissed her firmly. Lauren put her arms around Marc's neck and kissed him back.

Instead of placing Lauren's feet back on the ground, Marc started to walk up the flight of steps located to the right of the front door. "I want to show you the sunset from our bedroom." Lauren felt a shiver of anticipation run through her body as Marc started to climb the stairs to the bedroom above.

Lauren noticed that the house was unfurnished downstairs. There were hardwood floors throughout the lower level and many windows. Lauren could see the sun glinting on the surface of the ocean before Marc started climbing the stairs. As Marc continued forward, the light from below began to fade and the soft light left as the day turned to dusk outlined the hallway ahead of her. Marc turned towards the left when he reached the top of the stairs and carried Lauren into a surprisingly large master bedroom suite.

The sound of Marc's footsteps disappeared as he stepped into the room and Lauren realized that there was a plush carpet covering the floor. Sheer white curtains were draped over the windows and fabric overflowed onto the floor. The only piece of furniture in the room was a large, king-size bed covered with down pillows and crisp white linens.

Marc slowly placed Lauren onto the bed and she sank into a sea of the cozy down comforter. Marc gently lowered himself onto the bed and began kissing her tenderly at first before slipping his tongue between her lips, teasing her tongue to meet his own. Lauren could feel her body melting as Marc slipped his hands under her sweater and cupped her firm breasts. Their lovemaking was slow and sensual as the sun slipped below the surface of the ocean outside.

•

Lauren rolled over and looked at the clock on her bedside table. Most of her furniture and belongings had already been packed and removed from her small apartment over to her new home. It was almost six in the morning. The twelve hours before her wedding seemed to stretch before her. She could hardly wait. She'd been trying to sleep unsuccessfully for the last hour and she realized that sleep would be impossible.

Lauren and Marc had agreed not to run on the morning of their wedding day. They laughed about the traditions of weddings, but Marc agreed he wouldn't see Lauren until their wedding. She'd even agreed at her bridal shower to have ribbons strung through a paper plate to create a bouquet for the rehearsal dinner.

Lauren had laughed with Marc when she told him of her wedding shower. Lauren was convinced Mariana had sabotaged several of the ribbons that "broke" when she was opening her gifts. Marc had laughed when he heard about the prediction of their five children. "Five broken ribbons!? I better start taking my vitamins now."

Lauren cuddled deeper into her covers and enjoyed the last few quiet moments of her morning. Buster had been curling up at her feet during the past few nights and Lauren thought all the packing had made him uneasy.

"Don't worry, Buster. I'm not leaving you behind. Just wait until you see your new yard." Buster answered her with a nonchalant stretch and a deep rumbling purr that seemed to say that Buster had no concerns.

The next twelve hours that Lauren had thought would drag on forever were a whirlwind of activity. Never in Lauren's wildest dreams had she thought she would be so pampered. Mariana had arranged for a stylist to come to Lauren's home and prepare her hair and makeup.

Later, in the bride's dressing room, as Lauren stepped into her wedding dress and her mother helped her fasten all the little buttons, she looked into the mirror in front of her. She almost didn't recognize her own reflection.

Lauren had chosen a long, winter white dress with lace sleeves and a slender bodice. The fabric was formfitting to her hips and there were cascading layers of sheer chiffon that wisped around her delicate pearl colored pumps. They had decided on an outdoor wedding and Lauren had been careful not to select a dress with a long train that could be cumbersome.

The stylist had swept Lauren's auburn hair up into a French twist and her veil was covered with small pearls. Lauren hoped Marc would like the way she looked. It was so different than anything she'd ever worn around him before.

"There you go, honey. Every button is fastened," Helen Evans broke through her reverie.

Lauren suddenly became aware of Mariana who was sitting on the couch. "Are you alright?" she asked, concerned for her friend.

Mariana hiccupped silently before answering. "You look so beautiful. I think I'm going to be crying all night long."

Mariana was wearing a sea foam green dress that accented the blond highlights in her hair. Lauren had decided to have Mariana as her only attendant.

Marc's friend, Anthony, who Lauren found out owned the slip Marc used to dock "My Only Love," was going to be the best man.

"Well, honey, are you nervous?" Helen asked quietly.

Lauren had been concerned about being anxious, but as the wedding hour approached, her nerves became calmer and calmer. The thought of marrying Marc made her glow with an inner peacefulness.

There was a tap at the dressing room door that indicated that it was time to start the wedding. Lauren and

Marc had decided to get married at the Biltmore Hotel, along the coast of the Pacific Ocean.

Lauren walked out onto the Spanish tile entranceway and met her father. "You look stunning, honey," was all he could say as he took her arm and Lauren thought she saw tears glistening in his eyes.

Lauren squeezed her father's hand. "Don't worry, Daddy, I'll always be your daughter. Nothing will ever change that." Lauren felt her father squeeze her hand in response.

Mariana walked in front of Lauren and her father and Lauren felt her heart skip a beat. It seemed like forever since she'd seen Marc and she wanted to fast-forward through the song that was playing so she could join the man she loved. Lauren and her father had been instructed during the rehearsal dinner to wait for the beginning of Wagner's "Lohengrin" to start down the aisle and Lauren felt impatient.

After what seemed like an eternity of waiting, the music began and Lauren and her father started down the aisle. They walked parallel to the exterior of the ballroom and then curved towards the left to where the gazebo was located. After several yards, Lauren and her father made the turn that provided an unobstructed view of the gazebo and Lauren's breath caught in her throat as she saw Marc standing next to the judge.

Marc looked spectacular dressed in a tuxedo with a green paisley cummerbund and bow tie. Lauren remembered the first time she'd seen Marc in a tuxedo, the evening of their first kiss, on the dance floor at Lily and Leo's party and she smiled to herself.

Marc walked forward to meet Lauren and she felt swallowed up in his blue eyes all over again. Additional memories of their intertwined lives flashed before her. Memories that built the foundation of their future life together. As Lauren reached out and took Marc's hand, she felt complete. She felt like she was coming home.

Marc led Lauren up the steps of the small gazebo towards the judge and it took her a minute to register that the man in front of her was Leo. *Leo! There must be some mistake.* Lauren had thought that Judge Rollins was going to marry them. The Consumer Energy case had ended successfully for the firm and it had seemed fitting that the presiding judge marry Marc and Lauren. But Leo wasn't a judge and Lauren looked questioningly towards Marc and then towards Leo.

"Surprise, surprise, my dear. I was sworn in last week," Leo softly answered her unasked question before addressing the group in front of him. "We are gathered here today..."

At the end of the ceremony, as Marc bent down to kiss his bride, the sun was setting and rays of sunlight sparkled on the water of the ocean. The setting sun cast a hue of gold and mauve across Lauren's face and the pearls glistened on her veil as Marc lifted the sheer netting to meet her offered red lips. Too quickly Lauren heard Leo's booming voice. "I would like to present Mr. and Mrs. Marcus Harland."

∾

The reception the evening before had been a blur. Champagne had flowed, Lauren felt like she had danced on air and Marc had magically swept her away right before the stroke of midnight through a cascade of birdseed.

Lauren hummed to herself as she lay next to Marc, still sleeping beside her. They had escaped to the honeymoon suite at the Biltmore. Marc had escorted her into a waiting limo that Lauren had thought would whisk them away from the hotel, but instead had driven down the lane and circled around towards the back of the hotel.

"This way no one will know we're here," Marc whispered into her ear as he nibbled her earlobe.

Marc stirred next to her and pulled her towards him. "Good morning, Mrs. Harland," he said as he kissed her. Lauren snuggled closer and kissed him back. Life together was going to be wonderful.

Lauren and Marc had enjoyed a wonderfully relaxing day at the Biltmore before the bellman came to take their luggage out to the waiting limousine.

Marc had made arrangements for their honeymoon and their final destination was a surprise to Lauren. When he'd refused to tell her, she'd groaned. "How am I supposed to know what to bring with me?"

Marc had grinned. "I like what you're wearing right now."

Lauren had looked down at her naked body and laughed. "That isn't helping!"

Lauren had been able to get him to tell her that she needed "summer clothes and maybe a bathing suit or two," but other than that information he had revealed nothing.

As they walked out towards the waiting limousine, Marc put two plane tickets to Tahiti in his inner jacket pocket.

"Before we go to the airport, we have to make one stop," Marc said mysteriously.

As they drove along the coastline, Lauren wondered where they could be heading. They were flying out of the Los Angeles airport, one additional piece of information she'd been able to pry out of Marc, and the airport was located in the opposite direction.

Within minutes the limo was pulling up in front of the harbor near the place Lauren had met Marc to go running every morning.

"We'll be back in a bit," Marc said to the driver as he took Lauren's hand and helped her out of the back of the car. The driver closed the door once Lauren had exited and tipped his hat as they walked towards the harbor deck. "Take your time, sir, ma'am."

Lauren looked down at her sundress and stylish flats. She hadn't dressed to go sailing, but Marc was guiding her towards his boat. *What does he have in mind?* she wondered to herself.

"I wanted to give you your wedding present before we left," Marc said as they neared the boat.

As they approached Lauren realized that there was a cloth covering the back of the boat. Marc gave her a hug and said, "Stay right there," before he moved forward and pulled on the edge of the fabric. When he stepped away Lauren realized that her name had been painted onto the back of the boat. "My Only Love" was still there but now "Lauren," had been added above the original name.

"Lauren, My Only Love," Marc read as he took her hand in his. "I plan on telling you that every day, but I thought you should have it in writing as well."

Lauren felt tears come to her eyes. Then she realized that the harbor name had been changed from San Francisco to Santa Barbara.

"Anthony's gift to both of us is the Santa Barbara slip. We made the temporary exchange permanent," Marc said. "And, I'm giving you the boat as a wedding present. You seemed to love sailing as much as I did when we went out together and I wanted to give you something that will always put a sparkle in your eyes."

"Oh, Marc. I love you so much. You put the sparkle in my eyes," Lauren said as she kissed him with all the emotion she felt inside.

"I have a great idea. Why don't we finish this down below?" Marc said with a twinkle in his own eyes and he took her hand. Once they were below in the rocking hull of the boat, Marc showed his wife again how much he loved her.

ABOUT THE AUTHOR

Paris Tyler started writing romance novels in the 1990's and put the manuscripts away while her "day job," friends and family took priority. She's excited to get back to her creative life with the publication of her first novel, RUNNING FROM LOVE. Her next novel, ACT OF LOVE, will be available later this year.

ABOUT THE COVER ARTIST

Sam Mayle is a UK based freelance illustrator. He graduated from Colchester Institute with a degree in Graphic Design. He's been drawing and doodling since he could hold a pen and is influenced by sci-fi, fantasy and everyday life. He works in the London/Essex area. To see a video of the RUNNING FROM LOVE cover creation, visit http://bit.ly/2duNqsB.

For more information about Paris Tyler and Love Swan Books, please visit www.loveswanbooks.com or email info@loveswanbooks.com.